Queen of Hearts

James Love

Queen of Hearts

First Edition.

Published 2018
TNW Creations
Austin, Texas
www.tnwcreations.com

ISBN/SKU: 9781732300903

ISBN-13: 978-1-7323009-0-3

Printed in the United States of America

DEDICATION

I want to thank my wife for supporting my effort through the many, many hours the writing took. She listened while I argued with myself about what my characters would do. Without the suggestions of TNW Publications, the story would not have flowed as well as it does.

PREFACE

Terence Rodgers, private investigator, lives in the city of Canaan, in the imaginary state of North Colorado. Born in 1930, he once had a great career. He came to believe that Life, with a capital, "L," conspired against him and he became disillusioned in the mid-sixties. Now, in 1986, he merely goes through the motions. His life is like his office, outdated, tired, and in need of major reworking. An angry uncle, a missing heiress, and a young amnesiac with green eyes are about to shake up his somnambulistic routine. In the card game of life every man needs a Queen of Hearts.

Contents

PREFACE
Queen of Hearts 9

CHAPTER ONE
Page 14

CHAPTER TWO
Page 29

CHAPTER THREE
Page 35

CHAPTER FOUR
Page 59

CHAPTER FIVE
Page 72

CHAPTER SIX
Page 79

Contents

CHAPTER SEVEN
Page 94

CHAPTER EIGHT
Page 107

CHAPTER NINE
Page 120

CHAPTER TEN
Page 126

CHAPTER ELEVEN
Page 133

CHAPTER TWELVE
Page 139

CHAPTER THIRTEEN
Page 148

Contents

CHAPTER FOURTEEN
Page 164

CHAPTER FIFTEEN
Page 173

CHAPTER SIXTEEN
Page 186

CHAPTER SEVENTEEN
Page 190

CHAPTER EIGHTEEN
Page 203

CHAPTER NINETEEN
Page 212

CHAPTER TWENTY
Page 224

Contents

CHAPTER TWENTY-ONE
Page 232

CHAPTER TWENTY-TWO
Page 241

CHAPTER TWENTY-THREE
Page 247

CHAPTER TWENTY-FOUR
Page 261

CHAPTER TWENTY-FIVE
Page 272

CHAPTER TWENTY-SIX
Page 277

BIOGRAPHY
James Love 289

CHAPTER

ONE

Terence Rodgers heard the insistent ringing of his phone on the other side of the office door. He clenched his morning cup of coffee in one hand and fumbled for his keys with the other.

The answering machine cut in, "You've reached Confidential Investigations. Our secretary has stepped away from her desk for a moment. Please leave your name and number, and Mr. Rodgers will call you at his first opportunity." His secretary had, "just stepped away from her desk" two years ago. Something about him not paying her made her leave. The office wasn't generating enough income to entertain the notion of hiring another one. That's when he bought the answering machine.

Since then, he would occasionally hire someone, but the money usually ran out after a week or two.

He realized that it wasn't likely that a prospective client would leave more than a telephone number. Most simply hung up. Today, he got lucky. As he was unlocking the door he heard a male voice "Mr. Rodgers, please, call Mrs. Wiresmith at 555-1739." Terry Rodgers was due for a little luck.

By the time he got to the phone, the caller had already hung up. He decided to wait about five minutes to call back. Otherwise, it wouldn't look like he had been busy, since busy was the one thing he wasn't.

He walked past the empty desk with its phone and a blank appointment calendar. "1985," he observed, "only one year out of date." He noticed that everything needed dusting. "I'll get to that, later." he thought. Later, in his experience... would never come. He entered his private office, the office he had opened in the fifties.

His desk, one of those heavy wooden models faced the door. His elementary school teacher would have told him to rotate it ninety degrees so that the light from the arched window would come over his left shoulder. On his desk sat his old Underwood typewriter and a Rolodex that held numbers vital to his business. He never referred to it. He had memorized all of them and kept it more as a prop than anything else. Although in the past, his secretaries had needed it.

His filing cabinets were oak and like his desk, had been purchased when the local Air Force base was decommissioned back in the fifties. His telephone reflected the same vintage. He had moved the old leather sofa from his office to the reception area. That way the light from the window didn't interfere with the naps he had been taking lately. Normally he described his office as, "worn in and comfortable."

Today, he admitted it was just worn out. His office reflected how he felt about himself. For the last two decades, he had been whittling away at his self-esteem until there was nothing left except a sham of a man. When he had opened his office about thirty years ago, this part of town was a prosperous section. Back then he had been prosperous, too.

The years had passed and so had prosperity, so had any real hope he had about life. He felt like a dry, bitter husk of a man. Nothing about his job excited him anymore. It started twenty years ago and grew worse each year. For the last three years, his dedication to any case hovered at minimal. To his way of thinking, two words described him: failure and fraud.

He barely hung on to his business, to his life. Maybe the time had come to hang it up and get a job at Ace Hardware or learn to say "Do you want fries with that?" On his desk, the bronze horse with a clock in its side that he had bought when he wanted to grow up and be Roy Rogers showed it was time to call Mrs. Wiresmith. He dialed the number and after exactly three rings a very proper butler voice answered. "Wiresmith residence, may I help you?"

"This is Terence Rodgers of Confidential returning Mrs. Wiresmith's call." He hoped that he sounded professional enough instead of desperate for a job.

"Mrs. Wiresmith wants you to come to her home to discuss finding her granddaughter. The address is 22195 North Cherry Street.

When may we expect you?" The question seemed more like an unrefusable summons than a polite inquiry.

Terence waited a moment, and replied, "I have to finish some reports, but if I rearrange some other work, I should be able to be there between eleven and eleven thirty." In actuality, he only had one case: a concerned father, Mr. Ford wanted him to do a background check on his daughter's college boyfriend. The background check had taken all of thirty minutes. Brad Overstreet made white bread look exciting. The boy's life bored him so much that he fell asleep researching him. All that was left was to type up the report. He could do it in five minutes, but with embellishments, it might take fifteen.

The Voice simply said, "Very well. We will expect you promptly at eleven." and hung up. Terry's former English teacher might say the person hung up, but the dismissive feeling of the call left him with the impression that the voice hung up. Something about that voice chafed him. The report he had to finish for Mr. Ford might get the Voice out of his head.

He got up and went to the bathroom on the right-hand side of the room and opened the medicine cabinet that was above the old, porcelain sink hanging on the wall. His favorite mouthwash, anything alcoholic, was almost empty. "I guess the office account will have to spring for another bottle of Jim Beam." and he downed the last swig and dropped the bottle in the wastepaper basket next to his desk. The bottle made an all too familiar "clunk" when it hit bottom.

Work wouldn't wait any longer. Terry got out the typing paper and carbons to type up the report. All he needed to tell the father was that the young man seemed nice and had nothing in his past worse than an overdue library book. The only thing that was a negative was his uncle and you can't pick your relatives. Terry had found out that as an executive with the local Teamsters' union, the man had met with some people with ties to organized crime. A report that bland does not inspire someone to pay their bill, much less, recommend the writer to someone else.

The boyfriend's family made sure that they distanced themselves from his uncle. They distanced themselves from any hint of impropriety. He finished the report with a bit more flourish so it looked like it was worth the fifty dollars he was charging Ford. He accentuated the uncle's reputed connection with organized crime, a rumor that was never proved. Terry didn't care whether the report presented a true picture or not. Caring and ethics were luxuries the apathetic couldn't afford, and, when it came to apathy, he was president of that club.

"Be on time, but not too early," was something on old detective had told him. On time could be problematic. If he had the money, he would have taken a cab. The absence of cash meant he had to take his car. His car, a 1964 Pontiac Le Mans, had become as unreliable as his bank account. When he first got it, he dubbed it the "Red Rocket." Even now, it had no dents or real damage to speak of. Although now, it was red only in places that weren't rusty, even though the rust was only on the surface. The car had a certain caprice about when it would and wouldn't run. Only the relationship between owner and car and a lot of sweet talking kept it running. He thought about running by his apartment and putting on something besides his customary tee shirt and jeans, but decided against it. He could always say that he was dressed for a case that he was on. He decided on leaving in time to be there just before eleven. He could use the job. Even leaving in time to arrive early, he arrived at eleven thirty-five. An accident had snarled up traffic and a long, slow train did the rest. It wasn't all bad. Making the Voice wait gave him a smug sense of one-upmanship.

The Wiresmith estate was one of the older homes, with a capital "H," moneyed estates, in one of the elite neighborhoods of Canaan. He drove up the perfectly manicured horseshoe drive and parked in front. The lawn was pristine. Flower beds and roses gave a Fourth of July explosion of color. Ionic columns held up the roof to the porch which acted as the floor for the second story balcony. The carved mahogany doors were flanked by beautiful lead glass windows. Polished brass numbers boldly proclaimed the address. The front porch had four Brumby rockers each paired with a cast iron table. Everything about this place elegantly stated, "wealth." He resented such opulence. It reminded him of his failures. He went to the door, and instead of ringing the bell, he knocked on the door.

A solemn-faced man in his late forties or early fifties opened the door and stated, "Mrs. Wiresmith is waiting in the salon." The disembodied phone Voice now had a face; maybe it even had a name.

The butler led him into the room on the right of the foyer. Terry didn't know what he was expecting, maybe something Art Deco or possibly a dark Victorian. The room caught him by surprise. The decor was bright and very modern; sitting in one of those impossible pretzel chairs was a woman in her seventies, a youthful seventies, and still possessed an air of beauty. Obviously, she kept herself physically fit. She was dressed in a business suit, power blue, just like the magazines suggest.

Instead of a demur grandmother, this woman looked as though she could handle the toughest corporate board room in existence. She looked at him, pointed to a chair across the coffee table from her and turned to the butler. "Charles, some tea for Mr. Rodgers." Now the voice has a face AND a name.

She paused for a moment as if waiting for Terry to say something, then she leaned forward to make him think she had taken him into her confidence. He, too, leaned forward.

She began, "Mr. Rodgers, I value my time, so I won't waste yours." The subtle barb did not escape his notice. "My husband left our granddaughter a comfortable trust fund. Unfortunately, they had a words just months before his death. Each said some horrible things to the other, in the heat of anger."

She stopped her statement, looked at Terry as if expecting some comment, then as she poured some tea, she asked "Sugar or cream? I like mine English style."

"Just black," then he took the teacup and matching saucer and leaned back in the chair. "You were telling me about your granddaughter's trust fund."

Immediately, she returned to her story. "He added a proviso to the trust that if she didn't visit either this house or his grave within two years of his death, the monies in trust would revert to his estate. The first year, my letters to her came back. I've tried to find her through family, but to no avail." She dabbed a tear from her eye with a French lace handkerchief.

"There are only three months left and I am desperate to find her. I need you to bring her here so we can verify she has visited and attain her legacy." She paused as if she Terry was supposed to say something. "You'll need a picture. Unfortunately, the only one I have is about six years old and was taken before prom. Her mother sent it to me." Terry wondered why the mother wouldn't know where her daughter might be or why she wasn't mentioned in the trust. Before he could ask, she sensed his question and said, "Poor Amanda! Imagine losing your mother six months after your high school graduation." She dabbed another tear away. She added, "Cancer."

The picture showed a sixteen-year-old girl trying hard to look twenty-five. The make-up was a bit too garish and the face too young.

Still, she had all the promise of being a real knock out. His only comment was "A pretty young lady."

Mrs. Wiresmith straightened a bit in her chair and seemed to want to put his comment in its proper perspective, "All the women in my family are known for their looks. The plainest of them are still pretty; the rest are beautiful. She is beautiful. But enough of that; let's talk about your fees."

Terry had been thinking about his fees if he got the job. If he could carry it off, he might get five or six hundred dollars for this. Finding someone usually took him three or four days, if he got enough information. He could usually do it in a week if he had nothing but a picture or a last known location.

"Well, ma'am, I get fifty dollars the first hour and twenty-five for every hour after that—and expenses. I require two day's wages up front with any remainder being returned to you. You will receive an itemized bill when the job is done."

Terry noticed that Charles had returned and he tried to hand the butler the cup and saucer. Mrs. Wiresmith waved him away. A thought nagged at the back of Terry's mind. The household of this size should have had more servants. Perhaps he had overestimated Wiresmith's wealth or maybe it was the staff's day off. Something just didn't seem right. He involuntarily looked around, seeking something to which he could attach his misgivings.

Mrs. Wiresmith waved her hand, "Nonsense, much too complicated. I shall advance you a thousand dollars as a retainer of sorts. If you find her before it is used up, keep the residual. If you need more, let me know. I must find my granddaughter." Charles appeared with a checkbook. She filled it out and handed him the check. He made sure that he didn't seem too eager or too blasé. The deal had a suspicious air about it to him but the money looked too good to pass up. Nothing so deodorizes a fishy deal as cold, hard cash has a way of doing.

He took a sip of his tea and replaced the cup in its matching saucer. "Why don't we get down to business?" He pulled a notebook from inside his jacket. "What can you tell me about your granddaughter?"

His client's hand shook and she had to steady it with her other to keep the tea from sloshing out of her cup. "Her name is Amanda Jane Setrap, but everyone calls her Bandy."

He made the notation. "What about her height, weight, that sort of thing?" Mrs. Wiresmith pulled in a deep breath. "Let me see. " She closed her eyes as if pulling memories to the surface of the mind. "She's five-three or five-five and I have no idea of her weight. Her hair color changes with her whims. I can't remember exactly, but I believe it was an ash blonde. Her eyes are normally blue, but she does wear colored contacts. She'll be twenty-three in June, and she does like her social life.

That's not a lot to go on. He kept his thoughts to himself. "I'll see what I can do, and with any luck, I should find something to report on in a week or two."

After the usual pleasantries, he left. He ruminated on what he had seen. The house seemed more like a museum or art gallery. He had not noticed a single family picture. Neither had there been any evidence of anyone's taste except for Mrs. Wiresmith's. He might have his misgivings but the thousand in his pocket put a lot of them to sleep.

The thousand in his pocket wouldn't stay there long. His checking account and his landlord would get the lion's share of the retainer to bring his rent up to date. Still, a hundred found its way into his special "office account," the one he kept in his hip pocket. "I'll get a Mr. Coffee to replace the one that burned out a couple of years ago." Maybe, his luck was changing. He forgot the old saying, "Not all change is progress, just like all move-ment is not forward."

CHAPTER

TWO

Mr. Ford turned the report over in his hands. He didn't like his daughter Susan going out with anyone with ties to organized crime. He didn't care if she was a college student, now. She was still his daughter. He would protect her as best he could. Even if it was against her wishes. That's what fathers do.

He showed her the report and told her that he refused to let her see Brad again. They had a huge blow up about it. She ended it by running to her room and slamming her door. The first thing she did was call Brad. She told him about how her father had hired someone to check up on him and what the report contained. She said that her father was totally unfair and that his uncle had ruined their lives but not their love. Brad spent some time trying to calm her down. The more he calmed her down the madder he got about this private detective and about his uncle. After they hung up, Brad, in the anger known only to 20-year-old males, stormed over to his Uncle Saul's office.

Saul Overstreet was a man who didn't get where he was in life by letting obstacles slow him down. As business manager of the local Teamsters' union, his workday had no hours, just responsibilities. His office showed it. A grand desk and expensive furnishing decorated his office. It looked like the type of office that the union used as a description of corporate greed and excesses. His desk, alone, cost almost three thousand dollars. The desk had neat stacks of ongoing work and union issues. His Rolodex held the numbers of important people. The numbers that no one needed to know except him, he had memorized. Saul worked with a lot of people. Everyone in a position like his did. Most of the people in the union and those who dealt with the union were honest. Others had connections, strong connections to the Syndicate. Right now, he was involved in some ex parte discussions with Stephanos Basileus. They had to reach an agreement in principle or there would be a strike. Saul knew the teamsters would back the strike, but it wouldn't be pretty or accomplish any great stride forward for the union. He instructed his secretary that he was not to be disturbed for any reason. In spite of his dictate, his phone buzzed. Belinda, his secretary, was trying to reach him.

Against his better judgment, he answered the phone. Basileus shifted in his chair as Saul took the call. He looked put out.

"Miss Harrington, I said not to disrupt us. This had better be critical... life and death critical." His voice expressed dissatisfaction.

A practiced professional voice said "I'm sorry to disturb you, Mr. Overstreet, but your nephew is in the outer office. He seems to be quite distraught about something. He insists that he is going to see you. I've never seen Brad this worked up about anything."

Saul closed his eyes for a moment to think. "All right, Miss Harrington, tell him to give me five minutes and then my time is his."

Basileus could only hear one side of the conversation. The idea that he was so unimportant that he would be shuffled out of the office didn't sit well. His thoughts were "If they want to strike, let them." He stiffened his back and planned to let Overstreet know exactly what he thought when he got off the phone. Basileus was gathering his papers and putting them in his briefcase.

Saul hung up the phone. He turned to Stephanos. "I'm so sorry Mr. Basileus, but it's my nephew. He is all upset about something and insists that I have to see him immediately. My apologies, but he's family." Saul gave a defeated shrug. "What can I do?"

Basileus smiled and laughed. Family he understood. He remembered one time when, as a young man, life conspired against him. His father had postponed a whole day of netting fish just to hear his problems. His father, a true Greek fisherman, told him "There is no problem that talk and ouzo can't solve." His voice showed this memory. "I'm Greek. Who would understand better about family? Of course, see him. Let me get out of your way." He waved one hand like he was dealing with a trifle when he said "And this matter," referring to the issue before them, "a little talk, a little wine, we can handle it tomorrow." Before he left, Saul offered him a hand-rolled cigar from an unnamed Caribbean country. He buzzed his secretary and told her to let Brad in.

Brad stormed in, the image of wrath and fury. His uncle just stared at him. His stare had the effect of water on fire. He waited until Brad had calmed down. Saul pointed to a chair and told Brad to sit down and tell him everything. He ignored his phone and its insistent lights while Brad had his say. He told his uncle everything that Susan had told him, almost everything. He accused his uncle of caring more about being important than he did his family. Brad knew that his statement wasn't true, but anger and love make bad filters for the truth.

Saul remembered being that young and passionate and let the firestorm and adrenaline wear itself out. "So, this report from, what was it? Confidential? Is causing you grief." He stroked his chin three times, a habit from a time when he had a beard. "Hmmm, I wouldn't worry about it. I think that I can reach an understanding with this detective. He might even issue a corrected report. Most people are reasonable when you talk to them calmly, man to man, especially when you lay the facts out before them." He said this more as advice to his nephew than to reassure him.

Saul decided that some detectives need to learn that it is very easy to harm people accidentally, especially when you report everything you learn, whether or not it is true. Being involved with the people he was, he would contact someone, and a lesson in discretion and consequences would be taught.

Brad went home feeling unsure about whether he had done a good thing, but knowing that he would see Susan again. Saul looked at the phone for a full minute. If he picked it up, things would happen that couldn't be stopped. He considered all the people with whom he had dealt in his business life. He exhaled a sad breath, picked up the phone and dialed a number that he had memorized. Camford was the man who could orchestrate what needed to happen. He had arranged things for him in the past. Saul wasn't worried about the cost. This was about family.

CHAPTER

THREE

She became aware of two things almost simultaneously. The light said "WALK," and she had no idea who she was. She slowly became aware of other people around her, as the crowd swept her away. Her universe was expanding exponentially, but the black hole of her identity remained. As she took in her surroundings, nothing looked familiar. She had two questions that needed answering: Who was she and where was she.

Once across the street she sat on the bus stop bench and glanced around. She was on the corner of Saratoga Street and South Dayton Avenue. She peered into her purse, saw it was full of money and nothing else. She immediately zipped it shut. A rising panic caused her breathing to speed up and her mind to race to no particular destination. She had no idea of what to do. I need to go somewhere and think. She looked around for options. She saw a nearby Woolworth's store. Shopping, even just browsing, would give her time to think.

Not knowing what else to do, she went inside and pretended to shop. She didn't want to look suspicious but the not knowing anything about herself made her feel like every eye in the store was watching her. In reality, nobody noticed her, not even store security. She waited until she thought it wouldn't draw attention and went to the ladies room. She entered one of the stalls, sat down, and counted the money. Most of it was neatly bound with money bands from the bank. It made the counting go quickly. There were exactly thirty-two thousand seven hundred and eighty-nine dollars and ninety-eight cents. The money confused her. Was it hers? How did she get it? She was frightened and decided she needed some professional help. She thought about her options: the police, a private detective, or a doctor. If she had done something illegal, the money would get her into trouble, maybe arrested. The doctors might have her committed. She decided to try a private detective. At least, she could control some things, if it turned out that she was in trouble. If not, she'd only be out whatever a private detective charged.

She went back into the store and bought three scarves, some eye shadow, two tubes of lipstick, and a bottle of red fingernail polish. "If I don't buy something people might be suspicious." Besides, something about having a bit of make-up in her purse made her feel like there was some normalcy in her life. She left the store and found a phone booth. The tattered phone book let her know that she was in a place called "Canaan." She thumbed through the Yellow Pages looking for a detective and found one located at 432 North Dayton Avenue: Confidential Investigations. The address was in the McCrary Building. The address of the building appeared to be nearby, so she decided to choose that agency and started to walk.

The day had a May warmth about it: the Sun making it almost too warm, the shade making it almost too cool. The young woman walked the five blocks. "432 North Dayton. 397, 399 Oh, I'm on the wrong side of the street." she said to herself. Across the street was 430 North Dayton Avenue. The small building had a sign overhead, "The Sweet Shop." She went in. A kindly face man who looked like a stereotypical Italian grandfather came out from the kitchen in the back.

"May I help you, young lady?" For some reason, Tony Garibaldi, the owner, didn't think she was in his shop because she was craving gum drops.

She was looking at the various candies. "Ah, no, I was just wondering, do you know any-thing about Confidential Investigations?"

Tony's smile broadened and his face beamed. "That would be Mr. Rodgers. A fine man." With emphatic, rapid chopping actions of his right hand, he continued. "Never lets a friend down. Why did you want to know?"

The woman looked out the Sweet Shop's window at the surrounding neighborhood. "I have a problem and I need some help. I saw his ad in the phone book and came but now I'm not sure." She started to chew the polish off one of her nails.

Tony came around the counter. "He can find anybody, and he is a good, honorable man. You can trust him. If you have a problem, he can find the solution. Miss, if your plight doesn't capture his imagination," He put an avuncular arm around her, "the look on your face will melt his heart. Either way, I bet he takes your case. Go see him. See what I mean." Before she left, he gave her a small bag of lemon drops. "On the house!" The woman left, still uncertain about what she should do.

She stood in front of the building staring at it, still trying to make up her mind. The building was located in the area of town that decades ago was to be the professional hub. The Mc-Crary Professional Building according to the cornerstone dated to 1927. It was three stories and built out of dark red brick. Each of the old, large sash windows were set in an arch. A white keystone accented the center of the arches. A grander arch was in the center of the front. Just above the arch, set in the brick was a slab of limestone with "McCrary Professional Building" carved deeply into it. A set of stairs with five risers went through the arch. Between the grand arch and the front door was a terrazzo tiled stoop. The design protected anyone needing to get out the rain or other bad weather. She saw on a third floor window gold lettering, "Confidential Investigations." Her mind was made up.

She popped a lemon drop in her mouth with an air of determination, opened the door and walked in. All of the offices could only be entered from the hallway. The hall was lit by what were called "School House" lights. The opaque white globes sucked the light from the bulbs and emitted only an unsatisfactory illumination. In front of her was an old, worn directory.

The stark, white letters on the striking black background had aged. Now the letters were a yellowed ivory. Their board faded to grey. Very few of the offices were occupied, if the directory told the truth. First Floor Rm 103 Hei ann Jewelry, Rm 108 Expe t Ty ewr ter Repair. The second floor appeared empty. Third Floor Rm 308 Confide ial Investg tions. It didn't inspire confidence. Neither did the elevator. It resembled the type one reads about in old horror stories or sees in murder movies. She decided to walk the two flights of stairs. The third floor was darker than the first floor, owing to the fact that two of the lights were out. She squared her shoulders, determined to use Rodgers' agency. A moment later she had located the door that read "Confidential Investigations Terence Rodgers, Detective." She noticed that the door was ajar, and went in. No one was in the outer office which appeared to be decorated out of some 1950s Hollywood movie, and a "B" movie, at that, even down to the black leather sofa with a cushion that had a rip in the cover. The office had an air of a deserted room, as though the occupant had simply vanished some time ago. Even the oak floors needed to be refinished.

Everything seemed to be covered in a fine layer of dust. No pictures or certificates hung on the wall. The only sign of recent occupancy was an empty whiskey bottle peering out of an unemptied trashcan near the desk and a couple of men's magazines on the table. She started to rethink her decision to come here, but here she was and in need of help. Straightening her back she marched to the inner office door, opened it and saw Terence Rodgers trying to figure the best place to plug in his new Mr. Coffee. She stood directly behind him.

"Excuse me." Her quiet voice startled Terry. "Can you help me?"

The involuntary jump he made embarrassed him a bit. Two new cases in one day. My luck has definitely changed. He turned around. "What may I do for you?" He hoped that she hadn't noticed that it embarrassed him that she had snuck up on him. Years ago, no one could have done that. She had an unexpected effect upon him. For a moment, time reversed itself. He thought "Caroline!," even though she bore no resemblance to that woman.

If she expected a Paul Drake, she faced bitter disappointment. He, like his outer office, gave the impression of being slightly derelict. His appearance was somewhat unkempt. He wore blue jeans and a badly faded tee shirt. He was about five foot ten or eleven. He looked to be in his late fifties or, more likely, early sixties. He needed to get into shape. His inner office was as austere as his outer one was. "He must have used the same decorator as the front office, right down to the empty whiskey bottle that he has tossed away. He is not what I need" may have been what she was thinking, but what she found herself saying was "I need you to identify someone and what they did." Her initial bravado faded and a hesitancy seemed to surround her.

The fear and uncertainty in the woman's eyes pulled at him. He would've taken her case for free if he hadn't needed money to buy coffee for his new gizmo. He was that broke. He did a quick assessment of her. She was five foot five, plus a half inch for her shoes. Her jade green eyes and cascade of blonde hair. He couldn't figure out why, but she had an air of fragility. He guessed that she was about twenty-five. Not rich, but she probably had enough so he could charge her enough to buy some coffee and something to put a little Irish in it.

"I'm here to help. Please, sit down." His voice had an almost priestly quality about it. He pointed to a chair that matched the sofa, even down to the torn upholstery. Tell me who do you need identified?'

The woman sat on the edge of the chair, not wishing to test the integrity of the springs. "Me." was her simple reply.

He thought "Oh, great! A nut case or a practical joker." His expression of earnest concern never wavered. He had to decide whether or not he was broke enough to take nut cases.

The pause before he answered seemed like forever to her. He gave her a hard stare, "I get fifty dollars an hour with the first day's pay due right now."

She didn't even flinch, but reached into her purse and pulled out a bundle of bills. When he saw the wad of cash, his pupils dilated. Her next statement had a flat, business tone to it, "I assume your work day is eight hours" and counted out four hundred dollars.

"There," she handed him the cash. "Now that the fee is settled, can you help identify me? I don't remember anything before I was at the corner of Dayton and Saratoga."

He thought, "I can deal with rich nuts especially when they pay cash." If he had any special gift in his profession, it was that people tended to trust him and think of him as their friend, a natural talent that had been honed over years of training and practice. "Of course, I'll help you," he said with the expertise of a con artist. "Some investigators would think that you were some type of wacko. Me, I think that you are worried and scared. I'm good, but I'll need your help. First, I need to see your hands." Her perplexed expression required that he explain, "I need to look at them to get an idea of your profession." As they touched, static electricity discharged and she jerked her hand back.

The next time, he was able to hold her hands. They were warm and soft. The nails looked as if they might have been recently manicured despite nervous chewing. Her ring finger showed no sign of whitening, so no ring. He gave her a benign look. "Great. I have what I need," and let go of her hand.

He told her, "Write down everything you know about yourself or even think that you might know." He took a legal pad and pencil from his desk and gave it to her. "And let me see your purse."

She wasn't confident enough to fully trust him. Giving him her hand was one thing.

Giving him her money was quite another. She had a lot of cash and this place did not speak of prosperity. She thought "He might be a good detective, like the man in the candy store said, but I don't know how he has managed to stay in business, Even I could come up with a better plan for his success." After a couple of false starts, not knowing if she should let him examine her belongings, especially with all that cash, she sat her purse and shopping bag on his desk and started writing. If she really has amnesia, she can't write much.

He took her purse and dumped. He looked at her. She was totally focused on trying to write something. When the cash piled out on his desk, his eyebrows went up and he stopped mid-breath, but the woman was too busy trying to think of what to write to notice his reaction. The only other things were the scarves, the nail polish, the lipsticks, and the eyeshadow. Rodger started to thumb through the money. At two thousand dollars, two things fell out from one of the bundles, a bus ticket stub and a receipt from Sears in Kansas City. He searched for anything else in the purse. The new purse had no personality, no bits and pieces of ordinary trash in the purse, what in the business is called "pocket litter," He knew this was the only time it had been used. The bus ride from KC to here would have taken several hours. He palmed the stub. It never hurt to have something to razzle-dazzle the client. He would have to find a safe place for the cash, though, and his office safe just wasn't safe enough for his comfort.

He took the legal pad. The paper had very little on it. She had made several false starts and scribbled them out. What there was, he could read later. He did notice the precision and beauty with which she made her letters. "The first thing we need to do is get this money into the bank."

A worried look crossed her face, "Don't I need a name, address and identification to open an account?"

Terry originally had thought about deposit-ing it into his accounts for safe keeping. He thought about getting a safety deposit box. It would leave no real paper trail because he could keep it all in his name, but she probably wouldn't be convinced to trust him that far, because a safety deposit box would give him access to the cash, but she wouldn't be able to get at it. If he was going anywhere with this case, he needed her to trust him. "If you trust me, we'll put it under my name, just until we find out whether or not it is your money. I'll make sure that you have access to it, as well."

Oddly, he didn't question the ownership of the four hundred she gave him. Since his bank was on Saratoga, they could just walk there. He didn't want to spend any of his cash for a taxi and he didn't want her to see the Rust Bucket. Even bus fare for two might have revealed the only monies he had were the large bills she had just given him. He quickly read the legal pad. All that was on it was "I'm female and I don't know who I am or where I am or where I'm from. I don't know anything before I crossed the street at Dayton Avenue and Saratoga Street." He tore the sheet from the pad, wadded it up and tossed it in his waste basket. "Don't worry about your name, until we find out your real one; I'll call you 'Sara Dayton' after the two streets you were on." Before they left, he took a Polaroid picture of her. They headed to the Commerce Bank of Canaan. The good part about his bank was its location. He could see it from his office building. Walking to it wouldn't arouse any suspicion from his new client. She didn't need to know how broke he was. Except for the money she had given to him, the only cash in his pocket was the feeble remnant from the check that he had received from Mrs. Wiresmith. He had used most of that money to pay some back rent. What he had left, wouldn't have bought supper for two. She wouldn't see his car that looked like a reject from a used car lot, with the paint that had been overcome by rust.

The Commerce Bank of Canaan, like most buildings in this area, had been built decades earlier. Its lobby was an older one, rich in marble with tellers behind highly polished brass grill work; some potted palm trees finished off the look of luxury. A security guard watched everything. He had the look of ex-military: ramrod straight, badge, buckle, and buttons shining, and creases in his trousers so sharp that they looked dangerous. Terry noticed another guard in a three-piece suit; he pretended to be filling out a deposit slip. Terry knew all the employees. Most of them gave him a friendly, but noncommittal nod. He strode to Mavis' window. Mavis had jet black hair that she wore in that "Dorothy Hamill" style. Her eyes sparkled like they knew the punch line to any joke someone told. A slightly risqué smile finished the effect. She was his favorite teller. The other people made him feel like a recognized cus-tomer. She made him feel like he was a major stock holder in the institution and still able to attract a woman.

She gave him a warm smile and a wink when he got to the window. Terry had gotten into the habit of always asking his balance before doing any business. She had it ready for him. "Well, Mr. Rodgers, here to make another deposit, I see. Two in one month. I just might have to run away with you to help you spend your vast fortune. How far do you think we can get on your one hundred four dollars and four cents?" Then she saw the deposit and it was more than the one or two hundred he normally deposited. She smiled and said, "Maybe, Tahiti?"

Sara moved up to stand beside Terry. Then Mavis realized that Sara was with him and not the next customer in line. Sara watched her, appraisingly. She had the look of someone evaluating a situation and wasn't happy with the outcome. Mavis wondered who the unfamiliar woman was.

Maybe she's a girlfriend, a very young girlfriend. No, as often as we joke he never mentions any females, still she is giving me the 'stay away' look. She must be a client. Mavis thought that, as a good teller, she should have noticed how the woman looked at her earlier. "Honey, we joke like this all the time." Sara briefly, simply smiled back, but not a congenial one. She didn't like the idea of someone flirting with her detective over her money. Maybe it was because she didn't know who she was and this man would find out for her, or maybe it was because he was depositing everything she owned. Whatever the reason, she felt that Terence Rodgers was her detective.

Terry noticed the tension and decided to do something about it. "Mavis, I need to introduce Sara Dayton. I just hired her to be my new office manager so I can handle more cases. Sara, this is the number one teller in this bank, Mavis Eldon. If you ever need anything, she is the person who can either get it done or send you to the person in the bank who can do the job." He added, to prove his point, "Mavis, who is the best person to see about adding Sara's name to my accounts and getting a safety deposit box?" He was certainthatshewouldpointtoMr.Butterfield,butshe told him "Mr. Gibson," instead.

The next step was to take care of the paper work on his accounts. He went to Mr. Gibson, one of the bank officers. "I need to add my office manager to the agency's accounts and finally get around to that safety deposit box you've been after me to get." He thought "office manager" sounded higher class than "secretary.' Everyone in the bank knew that he'd never let a secretary have access to his almost nonexistent accounts. A cocked head, a raised eyebrow and a hint of a leer was the only reaction the officer gave. Everyone at the bank liked Terry but they knew that his accounts stayed so low that he couldn't pay himself regularly, let alone a pretty, young "office manager." His "secretaries" tended to be on the young and naïve side. They usually stayed long enough to find out their pay was iffy at best. The bank officer pondered Terry's requests. "Mr. Rodgers is acting differently with this woman. He's never given anyone access to his funds, before. I wonder what's changed. The only thing he might have valuable enough for a safety deposit box was a sheaf of IOUs that he had accumulated over the years."

Sara's name was added to all the accounts and when they went in to put the money in the safety deposit box he thought for a moment and said, "You better keep out about three hundred or so for living expenses." Sara for reasons totally unknown to her decided that this Mr. Rodgers needed someone to help him. Right now she had control of all the money that had been in her purse that now laid on a table. She decided that she should take up that mission. Just before she kept out the three hundred that Terry had recommended, she dropped a packet of hundreds. Terry bent down to get them and missed seeing her returned two thousand to her purse. She had some plans of her own.

Once outside of the bank, he turned to her, "Since you are supposed to be my secretary,"

"Office manager," she corrected.

"...office manager, I'll give you the employee rate of twenty-five dollars an hour." He felt generous, plus he'd just take longer with the case. He told himself "She'll be happy because she'll think she's getting a good deal. I'll be happy because I'll be getting some money from her." It would have been nice if any of that were true. The reality was that there was just something about her. He knew that she needed to get settled, but she didn't have an apartment. He couldn't leave her alone, not in the section of town. She was his client, and his business and personal accounts needed a cash transfusion. Right now, she looked like his financial blood bank. Then he turned his mind to more practical thoughts. "Let's find you a place to stay. That's the first thing."

She corrected him again. "That is, at best, the second thing. I don't have any clothes except what I'm wearing and the absence of luggage makes me look less than respectable to any hotel clerk. First, you must take me shopping. Just add it to the expenses."

"For someone who didn't know anything about herself, she certainly has definite ideas." he thought to himself. The worst part of it for him was admitting to himself that she was right. He could see the rest of the money from Mrs. Wiresmith and a good portion of the money he had just gotten fly away at her need for clothes. She looked at this detective. He was slovenly, unkempt. To her, he appeared to be sinking in a sea of debt and was probably a little shady. She couldn't figure out why she trusted this man. He reminded her of a beagle she had as a little girl. Or was she just imagining she had a dog, years ago?

They went to a nearby department store. There were two things that Terry hated: one was shopping with a woman and the other didn't matter, because it wasn't ever going to happen. Occasionally, she'd ask his opinion of the outfits she chose. It was as if she didn't trust her own decisions, maybe it was because she felt unsure about who she was. The simple truth was Terry didn't care what she wore. This woman was nice to look at but he was too old to help her with modern fashion. After about eight outfits, he excused himself, "Just find a few things you like. I think I might know of an apartment I can get you." The saleslady raised both eyebrows and shot him a sideways glance, but said nothing. He excused himself to get change and call his friend. He found a phone booth, a real one with doors that closed, not one of those one that looked like an egg. No privacy with those.

He called a friend who managed an apartment building in a slightly better part of town. Gerald had a soft spot for damsels in distress. Terry had to convince him to let Sara have an apartment for a couple of weeks at far less than it should have been. On the phone he had told his friend, "She's running away from her boyfriend because he beat her up and she is desperate for a place to hide until she can heal up and get a job." He just hoped his friend didn't feel too sorry for her. He might just try to help her. To be honest, Terry didn't know that she wasn't running from an abusive boyfriend so maybe it wasn't a lie. Not that lying bothered him. It hadn't for years. He just hated lying to a friend. By the time he got back, he hoped she had finished shopping. She had... with the dresses and had moved on to jeans and tops. He slumped in a chair, rubbed his temples and forehead and went into a semi-comatose stupor which had helped him survive similar excursions, in his distant past.

Dresses, skirts, blouses, tops, jeans, shoes, undergarments: Terry felt that people in purgatory had it better than he did. Finally, the ordeal was over and he helped carry the bags. To his relief, she paid for the clothes. He had a plethora of packages and shopping bags. He didn't know what all was in them, but he was sure that the store would have to be restocked. He told her about the apartment and hailed a cab.

Along the way, she tried to engage him in small talk which proved difficult with an amnesiac. Except for telling her the story he had spun for Gerald about her background he said nothing.

For most of the trip he just stared out his window. Sara stared out the one on her side.

The cab pulled up to one of those yellow brick apartment buildings that were so popular twenty years ago. Something about the building said that it had been overlooked since then. It wasn't run down or neglected. The building just seemed forlorn. Terry paid the taxi driver and went to get Gerald. The two of them helped get Sara's purchases up to the apartment. Gerald opened the door and let the two of them in. The apartment was tidy and furnished with low-end furniture, cheap but serviceable. The living room had a studio couch that could double as the bed. Sara's bedroom was down a short hall. The kitchen contained a small refrigerator and decent looking stove that had been cleaned somewhat recently.

"Stay here until you hear from me. I have some things to take care of early tomorrow and probably won't be able to talk to you until the afternoon." He was thinking of the Setrap case. Before he left, for reasons he couldn't identify, he looked back at her and fixed her image in his mind.

Terry took the cab back to the office to retrieve his car. Tomorrow was going to be a busy day for Terence Rodgers.

CHAPTER

FOUR

Terry's alarm rang at seven am. Normally, he got up whenever. He hadn't set an alarm in years. His morning routine involved sitting around in underwear and reading the morning paper and eating whatever leftovers were in the fridge and washing it all down with a glass of bourbon. If he felt motivated, shaving and brushing his teeth came next. A tee shirt and blue jeans were his uniforms of choice, but not today. The buzz of the alarm relentlessly prodded him to get up. He showered and shaved and put on his last clean shirt and his only suit. He had a lot to do but his thoughts were still in bed. He made coffee strong enough to slap the brain awake.

Nothing in his refrigerator looked safe to eat, so he made some toast out of slightly stale bread. Then he got out a pad and pen; it took

five tries to find a pen that worked. He made
a list of everything he had been told about
Amanda Setrap and realized that most of
the preliminary work would involve going to
roadhouses and clubs. He flipped to a new page
and wrote: "Sara Dayton: alias, Known facts:
The money was from a bank. She had a receipt
from Sears in Kansas City and ticket from Kansas City to San Francisco. She arrived in town
yesterday, assuming the ticket was hers, on the
early morning Greyhound. She's well spoken
so is well educated. Did she get the money
honestly or is it part of a crime?" He under-
lined the last question three times.

He added to the list, "I should have her
checked by a doctor who won't ask too many
questions just in case there's some head or
body trauma." He finally remembered Doc.
Hunt, retired, but reliable, especially for a
twenty, under the table. He wasn't dishonest.
He just didn't want his wife to know about his
tobacco money.

Terry left his apartment and retrieved his car
from the building's garage. Normally, when he
had the cash, he took a cab and thanks to yesterday, he had the cash. Nevertheless, today, he

was going to get out, "The Rust Bucket." Back when he was a teenager, thirty-eight years ago, his friends called him the "Rocketman" after some science fiction character. Every car he bought, he called the Rocket. This car he purchased brand new in late '63. It was his pride and joy, his first new car. Then, after the incident in '65 and the subsequent turmoil it created he lost interest in the car, in the agency and life in general. Both the car and the man declined from benign neglect.

Now, today, for some reason, it seemed taking the Rust Bucket was the thing to do. He hoped it wouldn't continue its habit of having to be coaxed and sweet-talked into working. To his amazement, it started immediately almost as if it knew, it too, had a mission. The Rust Bucket caused no problems as he drove to the Greyhound station. The bus terminals covered a full city block. From the outside, the station projected an image of a cold, unfeeling institution. Inside, it bustled with the comings and goings of all level of society. A quick glance around and one could see happy reunions, sad partings, and working class people coming and going from a dream unfulfilled. He tried to find a place that might have people who had seen Sara arrive. The moment he saw it, he knew it was the best place to start. The station diner was still turning out eggs and toast for breakfast. The counter help was a young man who was sure to remember a good looking woman. The fatigue on his face indicated that he had been on the midnight shift at the diner. Terry looked around at the bus station employees. He was sure the young man was his best chance for information.

"How about a cup of coffee?" Terry asked as he took a stool in the more deserted area of the counter. The young man produced a mug and filled it up. "Coffee" was a misnomer. The brown stuff in the mug had only a passing acquaintance with a coffee bean and too much familiarity with water. Terry put on a friendly smile. "Mugs are nice," Terry continued, "There's something about them, white, heavy, kind of makes you feel like talking to everybody."

The young man acted very bored, "'Yeah, pops, whatever." Terry bristled at the moniker "pops" but still smiled and acted a congenial diner. "Hey, I was wondering if you've ever seen this lady before?" and held out the Polaroid of Sara.

Without a glance, the young man simply said, "No." Then he added, "I see people all day, so many that I don't see any of them." He continued to wipe the counter with a cloth of dubious cleanliness.

Terry sucked a breath through his teeth, "That's too bad because finding out about her would motivate me and when I'm motivated I tip real good." and got out a five dollar bill. That got the guy's attention.

The counter man stopped wiping imaginary stains and took a long, good look at the picture. "Yeah, I remember her, now. She was here about 6:30, yesterday, and ordered tea and a doughnut. But she was out of it, you know 'spacey.' I knew that she was on something. I told her "Hey, share the wealth, baby. She looked around like she was trying to find something. Man, her magic carpet was flying high. She said "Okay," and handed me a ten spot and left."

The young man reached his hand out towards the beckoning five dollar bill.

Terry said, "Thanks a lot." and put the five back in his shirt pocket. "Hey, man, what about my tip!?" fry boy called out. Terry turned around, "I'm a good tipper if I'm motivated, and frankly, you didn't motivate me."

He retrieved the Rust Bucket from the parking lot and drove to St. Ignatius to beg another favor from Father Peterson. St. Ignatius Catholic Church was another marvel for the city. The massive stones, quarried locally, created an image of impregnability. The stained glass windows were gorgeous.

Several financially important people in town had donated money for them a few decades ago. Sometimes, Terry would read the names on the dedication plaques. Between the religious images and the massive walls, the church gave the impression that it could withstand any worldly assault against it. Terry tried to find Father Peterson. He blew the horn and waited.

Father Frank Peterson looked his part. Tall and authoritative, he had eyes that seemed to pierce through facades and right into the soul. His voice was well modulated and sounded like a declaration from on high. He saw Terry, smiled and offered his hand.

Still, the father eyed him with friendly suspicion, "Terry, I know it isn't morning mass that brings you here. What do you need?"

"Frank," for they were old friends and on a first name basis, "I need to donate to your teen program." The priest considered his teen program the gem in his Crown of Glory. It was designed to get the gangs off the street and stop some of the young kids from getting sucked into the violence. Terry gave the father a twenty.

"And what is this benevolence going to cost me?" the priest pressed. "I just want to use the rectory phone for one, maybe two calls." Father Frank continued to press in good-natured persistence. "Would that be a local or long distance call, because if it is a long distance call, you may want to be a bit more generous with your benevolences." The priest was busy getting ready for the day and didn't have time to swap tales with his friend.

Rodgers pulled out another five. The priest stood impassively. Rodgers fished back into his wallet and offered ten. The priest took it and blessed him saying "May God reward your cheerful giving by granting you the object of your intentions."

The priest's rectory office had an old desk. The desktop held a Rolodex and a wooden box for index cards. On the top of box sat a rusty nut and bolt. In the center of the desk lay a well-worn Bible, its pages thinned and curled by frequent use. Behind the desk sat bookshelves with a library of ecclesiastical books behind it, many of them in Latin.

Above the shelves was an antique crucifix. Religious antiques were the only vice Terry knew about Father Frank. Hanging between the shelves and the cross were his "family pictures," those people who held a special place in his heart. Terry had seen them so often he no longer noticed them, even those he was in. The phone had the heft of those made immediately post-war. He dialed long distance information and got the number of City National Bank in Kansas City, the only bank there he had heard about. He sang "It's great to grow with the

City, City National Bank" while he dialed, that was the commercial he had heard years before when he was attending a Chiefs' game.

"Thank you for calling City National Bank. How may I direct your call?" the switchboard operator asked. "Dis is Father Peterson." he replied in a passable Irish brogue, "May I be speakin' with the president." He found that if you are going to impersonate a priest, an Irish brogue goes along way to selling the idea. I wonder what she'd think if she knew Father Peterson was black.

The next voice was the person with whom he really wanted to speak, the Bank president's secretary. "Yes, Father, how may I help you?"

"I wanted to talk to the president about a recent donation."

"I'm sorry but any requests for donations must be submitted in writing..."

"Ah, darlin', you're misunderstandin' my intent. I'm checkin' on one I received that has me a bit concerned."

The secretary apologized, "I am so sorry for interrupting you, Father, please, continue."

"You see," he continued "a young lady came in and gave us a sizeable contribution, numbering in the thousands, wishin' to remain anonymous. Like an angel deliverin' a boon from heaven she was. Now, we're a poor parish and the gift was in cash and to help the disadvantaged youth of our parish and we just want to make sure, you understand... that the money was hers to give." He, then went on to describe Sara to her.

"Yes, that does sound like one of our customers and the funds would be hers, but you might want to hold on to the funds for a week or so. She sometimes has these spells of generosity which has to be recovered."

Putting on his most perplexed voice, "Spells of generosity? Does she have some mental imbalance?" "Oh, nothing like that, Father. She was in an accident a few years ago and sometimes has attacks where she..." and she stopped talking, She realized she had spoken too much. "I'm afraid any information about our clients are confidential."

With a voice of grave understanding, he responded, "Don't worry your head about it. My profession calls for confidentiality, too. Twill go no further."

Her voice was all business, "Father, if you will give me your contact information, I'll have our president return your call."

"Of course, my dear, It's Father Frank Peterson, St. Ignatius Church" and he gave the address and zip code and telephone number. "and let him know the donation was for our teen program. We're tryin' to help poor teens escape the hopelessness fostered by poverty. I have mass shortly and hope he can call me back soon. God bless ya and have a miraculous day." With that said, they both hung up. He felt guilty about using Frank's name. To assuage the guilt, he slipped the five under the phone.

As Terry left the rectory, he saw the priest and waved him over. "Hey, Frank, I just got off the phone with a bank in Kansas City. I think they might call you back about your teen outreach program."

Father Peterson heard the "Rust Bucket" fire up and pull away. It gave a backfire as a parting goodbye. A few minutes later the rectory phone rang. "Is this Reverend Peterson?" a male voice queried.

"Yes, it is," Father Frank responded while he removed the five under the phone and entered it as an anonymous donation.

The president of the bank had done a quick check on the priest by calling the local police who told him that the priest was a respected member of the community, his teen program was genuine and making a difference with inner city youth.

"My secretary just informed me of your call about the donation to your teen program. I understand it was anonymous."

"Yes, it was, but I know who gave it," a slight confusion in his voice.

"I was busy on another line, so I missed your call." the president lied. "I appreciate your promise of confidentiality and would like to send a personal check for a hundred dollars for your teen program.”

   “God bless you, sir. I can assure you that as far as confidentiality and the earlier phone conversation, it will be like I never spoke to anyone at the bank.” the priest replied. Somehow he knew that Terry Rodgers had a hand in this and said a short prayer for him.

CHAPTER

FIVE

Sara woke up with the same feeling of being in a strange place that she experienced at the traffic light the day before. It came back to her, the detective agency and the man who ran it. "I sure can pick the wrong apple from the basket," she thought. She focused and could remember the address. When she got up and got dressed, she went into the kitchen. She realized that her detective might have taken her shopping, but forgot to stop to get any groceries. She grabbed her purse and decided to go his office.

When the cab arrived, she told the driver that she needed to go to the McCrary Building. On the way, she changed her mind and told him to take her to a shopping center instead.

The one to which the cabbie took her, he felt was the type that normally dealt with people from her economic level, from what he could guess from her address. His fare acted a bit strange, not dangerous strange; a might need help strange. Time and distance created money for him, but when they got to the parking lot, he couldn't' just dump her off.

"Hey, lady, I'll tell you what. You do your shopping and I'll wait here with the meter off. You seem new to town, I wouldn't want you to get taken advantage of."

Sara was touched by his kindness. "Are you sure? I might be quite some time. I do have a lot of shopping to do, for groceries and a few other things."

The man pulled his hat down over his eyes and prepared to take a nap. "Lady, when you finish, I'll be right here." He pointed straight down. As an afterthought and a joke he added. "Just give me a good tip." That was the best thing about being a one-man operation. His wife was the dispatcher and he was the work-force. He could do things like this, at least once in a while.

The stores in the shopping center were a hodge-podge collection. She targeted the woman's clothing store and the IGA. The woman's store had some nice make-up and perfumes. She bought the make-up she needed and some nice, inexpensive jewelry.

She had almost given up on perfume until she noticed some of the upscale ones, the type that women in this area would want but not readily afford to buy. The store used them as teasers. Women would come in and take a short spritz from the counter bottle and go away with the allure it provided. She bought the most costly one only because she liked it. She stopped at a little hole-in-the-wall pharmacy and picked up more items that she needed. On the way back from the grocery store, she passed an office supply shop. She entered and ordered several things and told them to deliver them to Confidential Investigations, for approval. The management felt in a quandary. They didn't want to pass up a sale, but the value of the furnishing made a pretty hefty risk. As they hemmed and hawed about, Sara brought out three hundred dollars. "Would a small non-refundable deposit be in order?" They made a contract. They would let Confidential have them on approval for thirty days. She went back to the cab. On the way she thought "I don't know who I am or what I do. Maybe, I really am an office manager, somewhere. Maybe, I embezzled the money." She decided that she'd cross that bridge when and if she got to it.

The cab driver helped load in her bags and asked if she was ready to go on to the McCrary. On the way, she had him stop at a liquor store for her. He wasn't too sure about that, but he trusted his first impression of her.

When they got to the McCrary, she thanked him profusely and paid the fare. Then, she surprised him; she gave him a hundred dollar tip. Kindness may be its own reward, but a big tip sure sweetens results. He tipped his hat. "My name is Jason of Jason's cabs. If you ever need a ride, give me a call."

She went to the offices and found them still locked. She went to 301 which had a sign "janitor" on it. She knocked on the door. An elderly man answered. He looked at her, trying to place her. "Yes, ma'am? May I help you?"

He spoke in rich, deep, mellifluous tones. She sensed a strong air of dignity about him.

She smiled. "I'm Mr. Rodgers new office manager, Sara Dayton. I just started yesterday afternoon. He isn't in yet and hasn't had time to get a key made for me. I was wondering if you could let me in."

The man reached down to his belt and brought up a large ring with keys. "Yes, ma'am, I can do that. My name is Artemis Franklin. I'm the janitor. If you need anything, just call me. I live here." He didn't know who this latest girl was, but she seemed different from the others who came through every few months and then left in a week or two. Even those girls had been absent for the last several months. He unlocked the door and turned around to leave.

Sara called him back. "Oh, Mr. Franklin, I know it is a big imposition, but I had to leave some things down on the first floor. Would you get them for me while I put away items?"

The janitor didn't see any problem and left to get them. Sara went into the bathroom and put some of what she had bought in the medicine cabinet. Mr. Franklin returned with the bags. He put them on her desk and turned again to leave. "Mr. Franklin, I'm new, so I don't know where everything is. Like these trash cans, I don't know where to empty them or where to find new bags. I can't find any cleaning supplies for the bathroom and the dust in here is so thick. I was wondering if you could help me get the office clean for Mr. Rodgers?"

Mr. Franklin rose to Terry's defense. "Mr. Rodgers told me to leave things in here alone, that he'd take care of it. I don't want to go messin' with any of his things. That's what he told me."

Sara held his eyes with hers. "I fully understand. I wouldn't want you to touch anything that's his, but the dust and dirt and trash. I mean, with him doing all of that, he loses time for his cases. I'll tell you what. Just bring me the supplies and I'll do it. That way, I'll get in trouble and you haven't gone back on what you were told."

The janitor was locked in mortal combat with his conscience. He didn't want to upset his friend, but he couldn't let this pretty young thing in her nice clothes try to do all of that work. Breeding and his gentleman's nature won out. "Miss Dayton, don't you worry your-self about this cleaning. I'll get right on it." By the time he got back, Sara had already propped the doors and window open. She was talking to the phone company about upgrading their ser-vices and a couple of delivery men were enter-ing the office. "She ain't like the others, that's fer sure. She's gonna make Terry mad, I bet." He'd keep an eye out for Terry. He knew that the man didn't like changes or surprises.

CHAPTER

SIX

Terry took the stairs to the third floor. He hated elevators. Taking the stairs and opening the stairwell doors were the extent of his exercise. The early part of the morning had been busy. He checked with the police to see if they had any information on Amanda Setrap. The only thing he found out was that she had once been involved in a fender bender at a place called the Blue Ohio. It was his only lead.

He opened the third-floor door. Where the stairwell door and elevators emptied, Artemis Franklin waited. Terry wasn't surprised to see him. The man lived in the building and was the only other occupant on the third floor. Since Artemis Franklin was the building's janitor, the owners had retrofitted suite 301 to be his apartment. It proved to be a mutual benefit to the owners and to Mr. Franklin. Although they had known each other for years, Franklin insisted on calling Terry "Mr. Rodgers or, sometimes, Mr. Terry," Terry would have preferred that he was called just by his name. Terry Rodgers sensed something was wrong. Franklin seemed agitated. "Mr. Rodgers, if I did wrong, I want you to know it's not my fault. That woman in there told me to clean your offices. She says I'm susposed to clean it every day from now on. Now, you always told me to stay out. You didn't want me cleanin' none of your offices. Now, I can do one or the other and do a good job, but I can't do both. Which one am I susposed to do?"

Terry wasn't quite sure what the problem was. He had told Franklin years ago to never come into his offices. The man hadn't. Now, it seemed that Miss Dayton had told him to clean it up. "I'm sorry, Mr. Franklin. The girl is new and should be here only for a few days. She didn't know. I tell you what. Keep it clean while she's here. Just don't touch my desk. How does that sound?"

Artemis sighed. "Just so long as I know what to do. That woman is something else. She's like grabbin' aholdt of the working end of a live wire. No matter how much you want to let go, she just won't let you." Franklin retired into his apartment still shaking his head in disbelief. Terry wondered if he were up to having a live wire in his office, even if it were just for a few days.

As he neared his office door, Terry became concerned. The lights were on and he heard voices and movement in the office. He knew that no one else had the key to the office, except him.

For a moment, he had forgotten that Sara was there. He heard what sounded like an argument. Peter Gunn or some other literary detective would have pulled his gun and went in. He didn't have a gun, so he slowly turned the knob and eased the door open just a crack. Two men were pulling drawers out of the desk. He was just about to slip away to call the police when he saw Sara in the office.

She pointed to a spot in the room. "Put the desk there and move the plant over..."

SHE WAS REDECORATING MY OFFICE! He mentally shouted.

That was the second thing he hated most in the world, anyone, especially a woman coming in and changing his work space. He threw open the door planning to lay down the law. The outer office threw him off balance. He used his offices as a stable unchanging point in his life.

Everything was gone: the sofa, the Underwood typewriter, the phone...

They had been replaced with two new easy chairs a small table between them and a coffee table. On each of the tables were magazines, not the ones he liked and read "just for the articles," but "U.S. News and Report," "Forbes," "Look" and even the Wall Street Journal. The desk had one of those new phones with the push buttons, a vase of cut flowers, and a new desk blotter kit. A couple of pictures hung on the wall. They were posters from the New Yorker. He could swear that even the lights were brighter. (No doubt, due to the cleaning they had received.) She was planning on moving the desk so that it no longer blocked access to his office.

"What is the meaning of... this?" sweeping his hand in the air with such vigor that he almost threw himself off balance, which fit with his mental state.

Sara gave him the type of look that the nuns used to give him, a look that allowed for no debate as it was just a statement of fact. "As your new office manager, I took it upon myself to make some positive changes. Your office said that you weren't worth hiring. Prosperity breeds prosperity. I read that somewhere, or maybe I made it up. Can't remember for sure. Amnesia, you know. Oh, my new IBM Selectric should be here soon."

He told her, "I called you the office manager so we could do something about..." He saw the workmen staring, "Never mind. I want to know just how you paid for all this. this..." his brain was sputtering for a word to use in polite company, but all it could find was, "stuff."

She smiled the benign smile that lets any man know it doesn't matter what he says, he's already lost the argument. "As office manager, I contracted for it." She left out the part about using some of her money that she had secreted away to pay for it. "And don't worry, with the increase in business, this office will be a big money maker."

Despair filled his heart. "I'm treading water, financially, and she throws me an anchor." was his only thought and retreated into his sanctum sanctorum, the inner office. Some might say that he fled. In his office were some old friends: the leather sofa, the Underwood, the telephone. Neatly wrapped up and tossed in his waste basket was the answering machine. He retrieved it and hid it in his filing cabinet. "Why am I hiding it? This is MY office," he muttered to himself. He pulled the machine out of the drawer and set it behind his desk, on the bottom shelf of a book rack and put books in front of it so Sara couldn't see it.

"I won't stand for it! I should tell her to leave my office." Words like "should" and "might" guaranteed such a confrontation would never happen; nevertheless, he sat at his desk and put on a facial expression of great perturbance, and called out "MISS DAYTON, I want to see you, NOW!"

He was determined to, to…he wasn't sure, but he was determined.

She walked into his office with a bright smile and a cup of Columbian Roast coffee fresh from his new Mr. Coffee and a box of fresh donuts. Only three were missing. The mug read "Terry: Me Boss. You not. That's why." She handed it to him. What could he say? "Miss Dayton, I told you to stay in the apartment until I could find out something about your situation. He looked at a spot in the middle of his desk, pinched the bridge of his nose, and much quieter said. "And then there's the furniture."

"You couldn't expect me to stay in the apartment and starve, could you? You do realize that after you took me shopping, YOU forgot to buy any groceries for me, so while I was out, I saw this furniture and I remembered your office was in need of redecorating and don't worry about the cost. We have thirty days to make a decision" The staccato burst of words didn't give him a chance to even respond.

When she finally took a breath, he interject-ed, "And those magazines, my clientele doesn't read that type of stuff."

"But," she countered, "We want them to think that you are the type of detective whose clients do." She couldn't explain it to him, but somehow she felt responsible for him, like someone should look after him. She looked at him. "You look nice in a suit."

Her statement disrupted the cadence of his thoughts. He took a sip from his cup, stalling for a response. The coffee was perfect. "Next time, make the coffee stronger." Next time! I just gave her permission to stay. He cupped his forehead in his left hand and shook his head. He didn't know how it had happened but he had lost control of his office. His life hadn't been turned upside down like this by a woman since...not for twenty years.

Rather than a reply like he expected her to, she didn't argue or even raise her voice. She stood there smiling and said "Okay." and a single tear rolled down her cheek.

"Uh... thanks for the coffee. You can go back to the desk... out there." He pointed to the door.

After she shut his door, he paced his office and found himself in his bathroom. He wanted

a drink. He knew he had finished off his whiskey the other day. Out of habit, he opened the
medicine cabinet like teenagers open the
refrigerator hoping, by some magic, food
would appear. The cabinet fairies had worked
overtime. There was a new bottle of Jim Beam
waiting for him. The cabinet had grown other
inhabitants. Keeping the whiskey company
was a small bottle of soda water, some aspirin,
band-aids, toothpaste, two tooth brushes,
shaving cream, and a package of those dispos-
able razors.

The rest of the bathroom was spotless. "Two
toothbrushes??" Then he closed the cabinet
door. For some reason he smiled. The day felt
good. He decided not to open the new bottle of
bourbon, just yet.

The phone rang but it stopped just before he
could pick it up. He heard talking in the outer
office. "Confidential Investigations." A pause
"Yes, that's correct, but Mr. Rodgers won't be
able to see you until next Thursday, at the
earliest. I can probably work you in at about
two that afternoon."

Clients mean money and Sara had just turned one away. He wasn't smiling, now. Even with her money and the Wiresmith case, he couldn't pay all of his bills. He threw the connecting door open and when he stood in front of her desk, Sara knew this time he was truly angry. He slapped both hands down in front of her and leaned over her. "Why did you throw away a client and tell him I was too busy to see him?"

She rolled her chair back to give herself some space. Looking up in wide-eyed apprehension, her voice had a slight quiver in it, "But you are too busy. I noticed that you are working on something for a Mrs. Wiresmith and my case and so that doesn't leave you any more hours. I didn't throw him away, he's coming in on Thursday and said he was grateful you could work him in so soon."

After that, neither one of them said anything. Terry stared down at her, glaring at first, then starting to soften. She looked up at him with fear in her green eyes. He noticed that she didn't seem to be breathing. The quiet hung like a curtain between them. Time stood still.

She didn't know what Terry would do. He couldn't figure out exactly what to say. One of them would have to break the silence. Terry finally decided to just tell her the truth.

"Look," Terry began with a voice of resignation, "I'm flat broke. Until yesterday, I was three months behind in my rent, here and a month at my apartment. In the last month I've had three cases and even padding the hours I didn't make enough for rent. I can't afford to pay you; I can't afford new furniture. I doubt I can afford a can of Pledge to dust the new furniture. Your money was going to get me out a financial catastrophe. Mrs. Wiresmith's money was going to get my head above water. I may seem to be on the shady side of honest, but I won't cheat you. I'll get your money back, somehow, and I can tell you what I've found and recommend another private eye."

He waited for her response.

The quiet in the office was the loudest he'd ever heard. I gave her too much information.

Time in the office froze, once again. After what seemed to be an hour but was only the time of a few heartbeats, she looked up at him. "I don't want another detective and I'm content just to sit here. It makes me feel that I have something to do." The calmness in her was more unsettling to him than if she had cried or yelled or stormed out of the office. That's what all of his other secretaries had done. "My other choice is to sit in an apartment and watch a TV that gets two stations and both of those so snowy you'd think there was a blizzard going on. Just go on with your plans. I trust you."

Gentler than he had spoken in years, he responded, "Okay, come in and I'll tell you what I've found."

He sat at his desk and had her sit opposite him. With the width of the desk between them he felt safer, not from her, but from himself. "It's more professional." he kept saying to himself. He pushed two pieces of paper across the desk to her. "I found this ticket stub and receipt in your purse, yesterday." He gave her time to pick them up and look at them. "I palmed them. I planned to dazzle you with my investigative prowess by discovering where you were from and probably a name. Someone at the bus station remembered you coming in on the Kansas City bus. He thought you were on drugs or something. I think the money may be yours but I'm not sure yet and I don't have a name. I think you ought to see a doctor that I know to make sure you're okay. All of that took me about two hours, two and a half if you count travel time."

He didn't know that being so honest would make him feel so bad. He waited for her reaction to his duplicity and comments.

"If I charge you for two and half hours, it would amount to sixty-two dollars and fifty cents. I'll call it sixty dollars and call a good private eye." For years he had been just sliding by, doing the minimal needed to get the job done. Now, he felt like a cheat and a fraud with this young, vulnerable woman sitting there, just looking at him.

The woman responded in an unimagined way. Sara brightened up. "You are marvelous!" Each word being punctuated by an enthusiastic pause between it. Her voice picked up its staccato delivery. "Less than one day and you've found out so much. Why, I bet, in another day or two you'll have everything I need. We could celebrate with a dinner out." She thought about what he had said about his finances. "My treat!" She had seen his bank accounts while going through his desk that morning. She thought about the money in the safety deposit box and remembered that she had a key.

Terry shook his head. "I can't believe I'm saying this, but I've got to work tonight. I'm going to check out a dive called the "Blue Ohio" for Mrs. Wiresmith. It might be a lead about her granddaughter. It might be nothing." Trying to find a way out of the conversation he added "As a matter of fact, I have to go report to her, now."

His concocted excuse was the only way he could think of to get away from this client. This woman is messing up my concentration. I need to focus on my cases.

Sara thought it might be fun to see how a detective really works. She knew a few things about bars. She wondered how she knew that she knew. She thought that maybe she could help him. Sara's response was "Okay. Then, it's a date. I'll see you tonight."

He wasn't sure what she meant. For some reason, he responded "Ah, yeah, okay," as he hurried out the door. He needed to get away so that he could think. For some reason, being in his office with that particular client made it difficult to concentrate.

"Too much change never helps a person," he thought.

Sara watched him leave. She decided that anyone who was so fossilized in his attitudes as this guy was should be fun to play with his mind. She may not remember who she was, but somehow she had a feeling that if she came on to him, he would come unglued. She would dally with his male ego and see how easy he was to lead. Some people might think it was malicious. She just thought of it as harmless fun. "No one gets hurt, just embarrassed. If they get bent out of shape, then they just need to learn to lighten up." She smiled to herself. She had plans for this evening. They involved the Blue Ohio.

CHAPTER

SEVEN

Out in the parking lot, the Rust Bucket refused to cooperate. The engine turned over, but it wouldn't start. Terry got out, opened the hood and stared at the engine.

Opening the hood of a car is like rubbing the magic lantern. From seemingly nowhere, two heads appeared. One of them was attached to an executive type, complete with three-piece suit. The other was a long-haired, mustachioed escapee from a hippie commune. "I thought all of those types had faded away with Nixon." he mused.

"The last time it was points" Terry offered, as he tugged and twisted on random wires. The executive shook his head, "No, I bet it's the battery." He was busy taking off the cell caps and checking the fluid level.

The battery might have been old as Methuselah. A hose clamp held the ground wire to the terminal and someone had driven a nail between the battery pole and the cable, but it still had plenty of fire. "No, the engine was turning over," Terry responded as he continued to stare at the engine.

The long hair was examining the spark plug wires and then moved to the coil wire and then to the coil, itself.

"I know," the executive stood upright and pointed at the fan, "it has to be the timing chain. That's what happened on my MG." He offered his best second guess.

"No, man, that ain't it." The long hair held a skinny wire between his fingers. "This wire broke off the coil. No fire to the plugs." He pulled out his jack knife, stripped back some insulation and deftly twisted the wire around the coil's terminal. "That'll get you there, but you need to get it fixed, real soon, man."

Terry thanked them both, closed the hood and turned around. Like genies, they were both gone. That's when he noticed an envelope stuck under the passenger's windshield wiper. "Rodgers" was typed on the outside. Was that there when I first got in? He had been so distracted he couldn't remember. "When you hurt people, expect to be hurt back" was typed on the index card inside. He turned it over two or three times but it always read the same. He looked around, half expecting to see some trench coated thug wearing a fedora pulled down over his eyes and standing in the shadows of the building. The only thing he saw down the street was a pedestrian who might have been that long-haired guy and an MG being swallowed up by the traffic. He started to wonder about the broken wire. Was it an accident or sabotage? Then he came back to the moment. Standing here isn't getting me anywhere and he had an imaginary appointment. This time Rust Bucket fired up on the first try.

Today, Terry parked his car on the street and walked down Mrs. Wiresmith's drive. He thought "This house needs a junker parked out front, gives it a 'working class ambiance.'" It would give the neighbors something to gossip about too. The house still looked like a cover from "Southern Living," but today a man who had to be the gardener was working around one of the rose bushes. He wore leather gloves and a couple of holsters hung on his leather belt from hooks he had placed there. They stored pruning shears and trowels. His pants had heavy leather patches sewn on at the knees. The pockets on his long, leather apron contained tapes, wires, and aerosols that gardeners used in a winner take all battle with bugs... all bugs. Beneath his tam, his face seemed to be made of leather, too. Terry guessed the gardener's age to be near seventy.

The side of the house was lined with rose bushes; he assumed the other side was too. They started off with white roses and each bush shifted slightly more to the red until the last one was so dark that it looked almost black. Although it reminded Terry of the color of the blood at blood drives. Further back, the man had planted some new rose bushes. "Your roses are beautiful," Terry commented as he approached. "And the lawn...This place is a showplace."

An appreciative smile slowly crossed the man's face, showing a mouth of nicotine-stained teeth. "You're right, and it's been that way for the forty years I've been tending to the estate."

Terry feigned interest in the plants. "What are these flowers?" The gardener squatted down next to the plants and motioned Terry to do the same. "These are Viola wittrockiana. Most people call them "Pansies." I don't know why people call spineless people "pansies," why these little guys are some of the toughest flowers you'll ever see. By the way, my name's Bill." He took off a glove and offered his well-calloused hand.

"I'm Terry Rodgers. Could I talk you out of a flower for my suit?" pointing to a rose on a nearby bush.

Bill started examining a nearby bush like he was looking for a fine wine. Finally, he snipped off a well-shaped bud. He had made sure the bud's absence would not interfere with the symmetry for which he strove.

Terry put it into the button hole on his suit jacket's lapel. Terry reached into his shirt pocket and brought out a pack of L&Ms and offered the man one. Terry didn't smoke but he carried matches and a pack of cigarettes with him. Old habits, like lighting a date's smoke die hard. They came in useful, too, when he needed to talk with street people.

Bill took one and sat on a bench. He lit the cigarette and drew in one long breath. He motioned for Terry to sit next to him.

Terry decided to see if he could get some information from Bill about the household. "I've said it before your bushes are fantastic. They must win every blue ribbon imaginable for Mrs. Wiresmith. I bet she doesn't give you any credit."

"Aye, that's right. Wiresmith takes the ribbons with never a word of thanks to me. She tried planting a garden. She didn't know the difference between Narcissus and Zigadenus venenosus." He spit the words out. Terry pretended to understand what the man meant. "Working here now is not like when her husband was alive. He couldn't do enough to make people here love their jobs. Weren't unusual for him just to give the household servants little gifts or a gardener a bit of the grape. Since she took over, if you try to talk to Her Nibs it's been ' If you don't like it here go somewhere else." or 'You get paid.' If it weren't for fear of the harm someone else would do to my plants, I'd walk away and she could keep her money."

Terry shook his head in commiseration, "I know what you mean. I know this boss who yelled at his secretary just because she bought some flowers and rearranged her office without asking him first. I'd like to say he was acting like a first class jerk, but I don't think it was an act. As for me, no matter what I do, a lot of clients feel like I pad my bill and rip them off."

Terry decided to find out about dissension among the ranks. "I'll tell you who sets my teeth on edge. It's that butler, Charles."

Bill took another drag on the cigarette. "He ain't no real butler. He came her with 'Her Nibs'. Fires almost all the help, he does. Then," and the gardener looked around to make sure no one was listening, "he moves into one of the guest rooms, right there in the house, itself. He never associates himself with the help. Only three of us left, now, used to be eight. Miss Setrap, now, she was a sweetheart. She stood up for us. Tried to warn her grandfather what kind of woman he was marrying. They said some mean and nasty things to each other. I told her that she needed to go to church and ask forgiveness for what she said. It didn't matter if it were true or not. She just stormed off. After that, he just started getting sick and weak, and Her Nibs not seeming to care. I figure grief just ate up the old man until he just couldn't hang on to life any longer."

Terry shook his head and sighed, "That is sad. I know what you mean about the butler. I think he is a snob. I bet he thinks it would be beneath him to pick up a five dollar bill if he saw it on the ground. She seems to be a cold heart, too." Then, to seal their camaraderie he added, "What we've been saying stays between us. I wouldn't want, 'Her Nibs' to hear me talking about my clients."

Bill put a finger to the side of his nose to indicate co-conspirators, "Not a word from me will she hear." He finished his cigarette, stripped it and worked the debris into the soil.

Terry walked up to the front door. This time he rang the bell. The door opened and there stood a maid, about thirty. She had eyelashes that made sure you would remember her brown eyes forever. The rest of the package was equally memorable. He sucked in his gut a bit and wondered where she had been, yesterday.

He handed her his business card. "I'm Terry Rodgers and I need to see Mrs. Wiresmith." He wanted to make sure that she knew his name. As she left, her heels made clocklike sounds on the imported tile. She was nicely silhouetted by the large French window at the end of the hall. He hadn't noticed all of that yesterday with Charles. He watched her walk away and smiled. And smiled when she came back, too. Some sights look good coming or going.

"Mrs. Wiresmith said to wait for her in the salon. She said that's where you were before." She handed back his card.

"Keep it. You never know... you might need my services someday."

"I'll keep it, but I'll probably call someone else if I need any, 'services.'" She gave him a sideways glance, smiled and slipped the card into her top as she walked to the salon door.

Terry closed the door behind him, exhaled and let his profile assume its natural shape. I'm fifty, greying, and out of shape. The only person I'm fooling is me. Inside, he still felt thirty-five but knew he was really fifty-six.

Waiting bored most people. Terry was not most people. He used the time to examine the room. He noticed the pictures on the wall. Dadaism and Surrealism weren't his favorite styles but Wiresmith seemed to like them. Being a private investigator required that he have an encyclopedic memory. One case he had about ten years ago required him to know art. Most "art lovers" bought art as investments. When it came to choice pieces, she had four of them that caught his eye, a Tzara and a Tauber and two by Andre Breton. He thought, "There was more money on her walls than I earned in the last decade." By the time Mrs. Wiresmith arrived, he was down to checking out the details on the ash trays.

Today, she didn't enter the room but stood impatiently at the door. She wore a medium blue business dress, pearls, hat and gloves. "Mister Rodgers," He never knew so much disrespect could be tucked into a "mister." "I hired you so that I wouldn't have to be bothered I'm leaving for a luncheon. What DO you want?" He couldn't tell if she were angry about his coming to see her or just piqued because it interfered with her schedule.

"I thought you'd want to know that I got a hot lead on your granddaughter. I'll be going to the Blue Ohio tonight to check it out."

Suddenly, she was the concerned grandmother. The rapid change made the hairs on the back of Terry's neck stand up. "You do? You'll never know what this means to me. I'm sorry I was so abrupt, but these business luncheons are so important for later charity contacts. I'm sorry but I must go, even now I have to call to let them know I'll be late. Please, show yourself out."

She went to the phone and dismissively waved him out the door. Her last statement made him feel like the delivery boy who had failed to wipe his shoes.

As he stood at the open door, he saw the maid coming out of another room. She tapped her chest, "I've still got your card." and gave him a wink. He knew it was all farce, but at this point in his life, even the farce did his male ego good.

While he walked up the driveway, Bill ran over to him with a potted plant. "Here, you go. If you ever see that secretary again, give her this. It's one of my best Boston ferns. It'll drive her boss crazy. Maybe, you could even persuade her to go to lunch with you."

"Yeah, if she can ever get away from that boss of hers. You have no idea what a royal pain he can be to her." He took a few steps, turned back, "Thanks for the fern."
Bill kept his head down, focused on the new rose he had just planted and absently waved at him. He was once again "the gardener" lost in his world of green.

Terry started thinking about the money this case promised to bring him. Even the promise of a financial reprieve couldn't get rid of that nagging feeling creeping up his neck or the sense that he was on the wrong side of the playground.

CHAPTER

EIGHT

He was going to need some operating capital for the evening. Terry examined his wallet; twenty-seven dollars isn't going to cut it. He drove to the branch bank. The drive-thrus were busy, so he parked waiting for the line to thin out. "This will give me time to get the check ready." He hated it when he got behind people that did a month's worth of banking one unfinished piece of paper at a time. He opened his wallet and pulled out the agency check he carried. The check had assumed the curve of the wallet and the edges were worn. He had to do some mental calculations, "Cover charge, two drink minimum, tips, walking around money. Some money just in case I get lucky. Probably a hundred would do. Better make it one fifty." He ended up making it out for two hundred.

When he pulled up to the pneumatic tube and put the check into it. "I hope the account has enough to cover it." He gave the case a kiss for luck and sent it on its way. He crossed his fingers when he heard the intercom click. He was afraid that he would be told that his funds were insufficient, but all he got was a "Thank you, Mr. Rodger" and a whoosh that delivered the cash.

He spent the rest of the afternoon in his apartment. It felt empty today. Maybe, he was remembering Caroline, or more likely, thinking about the woman in his office. She had a way of circumventing him. She had a way of...well just a way. He looked at the fern. "You know I'm not hiding out." The fern said nothing. "I could go back to the office, but I need to be focused for this evening." The fern continued its passive listening. "Miss Dayton, or whatever her name is, just doesn't understand what it takes to do a proper investigation." The fern was not impressed even with him shaking his finger at it. "So, I am NOT hiding out from that woman." Terry knew he was lying. He feared that age and indolence had turned his abilities into inabilities. Years ago, no one could have snuck up on him like she had in his office.

Years ago, he would have identified what bothered him about Wiresmith. I'm like my car, I guess. All rust and memories. I've either got to get back in the game or get out. For some reason, since that woman walked into his office, he had started to examine his life. He wasn't fond of what he saw. He looked at the fern. When he said "And don't think I don't know what you're thinking." he realized that he was trying to rationalize his behavior to a fern. If anyone hears me, they'll know I'm flirting with the crazy side of thinking. He ended up giving the fern a drink of water and himself a shot of whiskey.

When the time was right, he left for the roadhouse. The old Rust Bucket fired right up and seemed to be happy to be on a case again, happy if one can ascribe human emotions to a machine. He took the old highway out of town. People had hoped that the city would develop in this direction, so they started building strip malls and laying out neighborhoods that no one ever built. The interstate and the threat of new taxes had killed any chance of economic prosperity. The Ford and Carter years drove in the last nails into those coffins. He kept driving past the half-empty strip malls and buildings that stood like abandoned dreams. He drove well past the edge of town. The only thing out this direction were two old motels that had become transient housing, an empty Gulf gas station with its original sign faded and rusting away, and the Blue Ohio Roadhouse.

When he got to the "Blue Ohio," the bar didn't disappoint him. The parking lot was crowded and in bad shape. The pavement in the parking lot was more of a memory than a fact. Where any attempt of repair had been made it was with gravel and a half-hearted effort to get it near the potholes. It gave the parking lot the feeling of a mockup of a lunar surface. The cars were an eclectic mixture of makes and conditions.

He parked his car next to sixty-three Cadillac. The Cadillac was in excellent shape. His red Sixty-four Pontiac was at the other end of the paint job spectrum.

The bar was a place where everyone was welcome, but no one could remember you being there if they were asked. The name was odd because it wasn't located near any water. The neon sign above the door read "Blue O io" with the "h" occasionally flashing to life. Inside, cigarette smoke created an eye-blurring fog that made the dim lights even dimmer. The air was heavily scented with Stetson and cheap perfume fighting for dominance over the tobacco smoke and beer. A lackluster band played non-descript music for the patrons. Some couples moved haphazardly in an imitation of a dance, while others sat at the booths and tables and ignored the sounds in the air.

The waitresses wore blouses that let any man who might want to check it out, see that moss doesn't grow on the north side of those trees. The crowded bar had two types of customers: desperate and lonely, each group trying to connect with the other. Off to one end, a woman in a halter top teased her date by paying way too much attention to the man next to her. Her date was fuming and pulling at her arm. Another man and his date were playing "ice cube basketball." He used his spoon to pitch ice cubes at his date's cleavage. The point was to make a "basket" in the cleavage. Apparently, the rules of the game were if he missed he downed a shooter. If he scored a "basket" she downed a shooter. He was a good shot and his date having lost most of her inhibitions made the target harder to hit by swaying a bit. The bouncer was headed over to "escort" a patron out after being signaled by a waitress who felt he was too friendly. The bartender had a winning smile until he turned around. In the mirror, Terry could see the bartender looking bored. For him, it was just another night. The actors changed, but the play was still the same. Terry walked over to him. The bartender wore a name tag, "Ted."

"Hey, bartender, how about a bourbon and branch water on the rocks?" He handed him a five. The bartender was back in a few second with the drink and the change which he laid on the bar. "Keep the change," Terry said. He looked at the nametag just to make sure of the name. "Ted, but let me ask if you've seen this woman. She'd be about six years older than this picture?"

"No one that young could have gotten in here." Terry slipped a ten on top of the ones. Ted's memory suddenly improved. He continued "but she does look a bit like someone who used to come in. What was her name?...Pammy, Mandy, Brandy, something like that." He scooped up the money. "That's all I can remember." Then he left to flirt with two women at the other end of the bar, one of whom gave him the eye.

Suddenly there was a tap on Terry' shoulder. "Well, you took your sweet time getting here." He knew the voice was Sara's. "While waiting for you, I've had three free drinks and four totally indecent proposals." She slipped her arms around his waist and clasped her hands together at his buckle.

He turned and was stunned. Her green and white outfit was designed to catch a man's eye. Her short skirt passed as barely legal and her top, obviously braless, showed off her shape and cleavage to her best advantage. Her make-up looked like it was put on with too broad a brush, but the effect was that for a moment he stopped thinking with his brain. A mental slap to his frontal cortex brought him back to his purpose for coming to the bar. He didn't like this upstart of a girl worming her way into HIS investigation. He pulled her over to a booth.

"What are you doing here?" He demanded in a whisper.

"Remember, we had a date." He pushed on her shoulder to make her sit down. "Ooh, a little rough stuff." She looped a finger around a button on his shirt and gave a little tug.

"I thought you might need my help. A woman can get information that a man can't." Sara took a sip of her gin and tonic. "I've been investiligating."

She sounded like someone flirting with the edges of intoxication. "When I found out that the waitress over there has been here the longest, I made sure to get her table." She pointed to waitress with twin braids that hung down to her shoulders. The woman appeared to be in an animated and slightly heated con-versation with the bartender. She started walking over to their table. "A waitress, if you can get them talking would be a great source of information, particularly about any woman who is a regular."

"Oh, really? And where will you get this inside information?"

"The ladies' room."

Their waitress, Meg, interrupted them, "The ladies' is down that way." pointing to a hall at the far end of the bar. An arrow had "Rest-rooms" routed in it and hung below an exit sign. This time of night, the patrons had consumed enough drinks to create a steady line of people using the facilities. The waitress continued, "Did you want to reorder?"

"I'll have a gin and tonic and he'll have the bill." She put her elbow on the table and her chin in her hand. "He always pays," and gave an exaggerated wink indicative of someone who wasn't aware of their sobriety or lack of it. She turned back to him and said: "That's four drinks, do you want to make an indecent proposal number five, I might say 'yes.'"

He hoped it was the three drinks talking. He decided that it was time to put her flirting to a stop. Besides, he found forward women to be abrasive. "I'm in my fifties, and you're half my age. You're young enough to be my own daughter."

"Or niece," she added. "But I'm not either, besides, look around. There are a lot of uncles here with their nieces. I'm not really intoxlicated; I'm just pretending for effect." Even if they were watered down, Terry could tell that the gins were affecting Sara. She asked him, "So, do you want to be my uncle or sugar daddy, this ebening." Errors kept creeping into her speech.

The waitress gave the bartender the order, "Table 10. Gin and tonic." The bartender noticed Terry with Sara and remembered the ten spot. He's not going to get anywhere with that hot babe without help. He made the bourbon light, and the gin and tonic was heavy on the gin and almost no tonic. For camouflage, he added a twist of lemon. He handed the drinks to the waitress and whispered something to her.

When the waitress came back, wiped the table, put down fresh napkins, with the drinks. She "accidentally spilled about half of Sara's drink. Terry felt trapped by Sara's behavior. He didn't have control of the investigation, and he needed that. He prided himself on his investigative abilities when he put his mind to it. Now, he was stuck. He could only play the role Sara had selected for him, playing the game of boss and secretary. He slipped the

waitress a five and put his finger to his lips.
"Shhh" and winked.

The two of them sipped their drinks. Sara
moved her head and shoulders to the rhythm of
the music. Terry just sat there. Finally, she
gulped down the rest of her drink, grabbed
his arm.

"If we are supposed to be a couple we have to
pretend to talk or, at least, dance. We're dancing." She hauled him to the floor. The dance
was a slow one. He wasn't completely into the
idea, but dancing had its own effect on him. He
could feel the warmth of Sara's body, and, in
spite of the smoke, the perfume she was wearing. It wasn't cheap. Nothing about her was
cheap. The perfume's scent found its way to his
brain and transfused throughout his entire
being. He closed his eyes and shut out everything else but the dance. As they moved together on the floor in sync, time and space
seemed to disappear. The movement, the
music, the smell of perfume, the sense of
touch, the warmth of human closeness were all
one. Maybe she took a misstep or maybe a note
fell flat but something happened to break the
spell. They danced on. When the song ended,

they went back to their table. On the way back, she said to Meg in passing "Another gin."

Ted created another of his high octane gin and tonics. This time he sweetened the deal by adding a little something special when no one was looking. The Bartender thought, "Now he can't help but score once that stuff gets into her system."

Meg brought the drink and tapped her slightly on the arm and headed for the restroom. Sara took a good sized gulp from the drink. She realized that Meg wanted her to follow. "I'll be right back," she whispered to Terry but added in a louder voice than necessary, "I have to go power my nose. Powder my nose." She giggled and wagged her finger at him. "Now you just sit there 'til I get back. I'm still expecting that proposal." She felt hot, so she undid one more button on her blouse.

Terry chocked her behavior up to her being someone who was used to partying without thought to the consequences. She needs someone to provide guidance, someone who will help her make better decisions. He scanned the patrons. He felt sorry for the types of people so desperately trying to grab onto happiness that its grains slipped through their fingers and disappeared into the air.

CHAPTER
NINE

Low wattage bulbs illuminated the hallway, and when she entered the restroom, its appearance should have had a sobering effect. The floor was cheap linoleum that looked to be cleaned regularly: New Year's Eve and the Fourth of July, and it was only mid-May now. Only great need would compel any woman to use either of the two stalls. The trash cans were over flowing with all manner of debris, and, from the odor, at least one of the two stalls didn't seem to flush. Both seats gave the appearance of a disease waiting to happen. The only thing going for it was a counter with two sinks, mirrors with lights above them. Meg was freshening up her make-up. Sara got out her lipstick. Meg took a paper towel and used it to get rid of the excess lipstick. Sara started to put on more lipstick. "You have a fun place here, but I don't think I'll be back. It's my bah...boyfriend." She wanted it to sound like she almost said, boss.

The waitress had seen a lot of women who stopped themselves from saying "boss."

"Look, honey, if he's getting too handsy and you don't like it, just let me know, and I'll get Andy, our bouncer. I wanted to warn you that your "boyfriend" and that creep, Ted, are loading your drinks. I don't care what people do here, but I don't like any woman to be blindsided."

Sara turned to her and felt a bit dizzy. That last drink hit her harder than any other drink had. Her brain felt fuzzy around the edges. "I don't want to lose my job. I'm his offlicer, ah office managerer. He's really a nice guy, but I won't be back with him, all he talks about is someone named..."

She had to think for a moment to remember the name. "Bandy. I don't want him to rum, ah, run into her." She noticed that she was having trouble forming words exactly. She giggled a bit.

As the waitress threw the paper towel toward the overflowing trashcan, she advised Sara, "Bandy hasn't been here in months, said she was going someplace where she'd meet younger men. And you can do better than your boss, out there. There no man worth breaking a nail over."

Sara interrupted her, "A college friend told me when it comes to men remember the three 'Fs.'" I can't believe I just said that. The alcohol is getting to me. Both women did a quick laugh. They left the restroom, giggling to each other. A few seconds later, when one of the men tried to hit on Meg, they exploded in laughter so hard that people nearby asked what the joke was, which made them laugh even harder.

On the way back to the table she had a hard time walking straight. That last drink was a doozy. When she returned to the booth, she was dabbing a tear from her eye, still laughing to herself.

"What's so funny."

She coughed a couple of times to get control of herself, "Can't tell you, it's a secret, but I can tell you this." She wiggled her finger in a come here motion. Terry leaned closer. With each syllable, she had spoken more softly until his ear was next to her lips. "Bandy hasn't been here in months. I think I have a lead. I'll tell you but not here. Too many people here and they all have ears, here." Then she did a spit giggle. "Ears hear, here ears." To her, it sounded funny. Focusing was getting harder and harder for her. She knew something wasn't right, but she didn't seem to care. Nothing mattered. The room seemed to be a merry, merry-go-round.

While Sara was gone, Terry had been scanning the room. No one looked like Wiresmith's niece. He caught the eye of a few of the women, but ignored them, mostly. When Sara was coming back from the ladies' room, she looked real unsteady, and that fact worried him.

He tried to stop her from drinking. Sara grabbed her glass and downed the drink hurriedly. "I'm at six and four. You are not keeping up your end. You owe me two indecent prolopsals" She held up her index finger and wagged it back and forth like she was correcting him. "One more dance and we'll go." She stood up and found she had lost her equilibrium. "I don't feel so good." The room started to move around her. "Woo, it is getting warm. I think I need some flesh hair, ah fresh air." Even in her current state, she knew something was wrong. Terry watched the rapid onset of her apparent drunkenness.

Now, he knew for certain that something was wrong. This was no ordinary drunk. He had seen plenty of those and participated in quite a few, himself. He tried to think of some way to get her out without drawing attention to themselves. The last thing he wanted was for her to pass out or someone to call an ambulance. At that moment, the young man could stand halter top's flirting no longer, took a swing at the other man. Everyone rushed to watch the fight. Terry walked a staggering, barely conscious Sara towards the door. Somewhere a flashbulb went off. In the ensuing chaos, Terry spirited Sara out the door and navigated her to the parking lot.

When they got outside, he informed her "I'm taking you home, immediately." and walked her toward the Rust Bucket. The job was harder than he imagined as she was having more trouble standing. Just when he got her to the back of the car, she lost her balance. He went to catch her as a loud kah-thum filled the air. The rear window exploded. He flung the rear door open. Sara was struggling to get up, but he pushed her into the back seat. Then crawled just like they taught him in the army, to the driver's door.

He crouched in the driver's seat below a shooter's line of vison, he hoped. He got the keys in the ignition and started his car. He sat upright in the seat, threw the transmission into drive and floored it. Gravel and dust sprayed behind him as he fishtailed out of the lot. As they sped away another bullet put a hole in the rear quarter panel. Terry focused so hard on trying to keep them both alive that he didn't hear that shot.

CHAPTER

TEN

The Bucket ran at speeds it hadn't seen in years and kicked out a cloud of carbon that had built up. He didn't slow down until he was well beyond bullet range and the bar was only a speck in the rearview mirror. The adrenaline was still at its peak. He felt eighteen again. "Woohoo! Rocket Man is back," he shouted, throwing a fist into the air, then adjusted the rearview mirror so he could keep an eye on the backseat.

"That's okay, baby," he cooed, as he patted the dashboard, "I'll get you all patched up and new glass, too." Terry's, "woohoo" had caused Sara to become almost conscious. Until he mentioned the glass, Sara, in her haze, thought he might be talking to her. Then she passed out.

He continued to drive west on State highway thirty-two. The straight stretch of road made it hard for anyone to follow without being seen. The fact that both sides of the road had deep ditches made sure no one could turn on or off the road.

The moon was full. He was driving without lights and praying that the roads weren't being patrolled. I can prove I was shot at but how can I make "I'm running from someone who isn't chasing me." sound reasonable? He was near his goal, an abandoned Stuckey's. From here he could see if anyone was tailing him and he'd have time to think.

The front door of the building was torn off its hinges, and one of the plate glass windows had been broken out. The side of the building was covered with graffiti. The gravel, broken bottles and crushed beer cans moved under his wheels as he came to a stop behind the build- ing. The back door was open, but he wasn't interested in going in, he hoped no one would come out. I can't go home until I figure out who's tried to kill me. I can't stay here, all night. Then he remembered a fish camp off a

nearby side road and the motel that was attached to it. He hoped the motel was still there.

In the backseat, Sara had come to. She
moaned, "I don't feel too well." She opened
the door and stumbled out. With all the broken
bottles, Terry worried that she might cut herself if she fell. He got out and ran to steady her.
He helped her to weeds that were encroaching
on the lot. She almost made it. She vomited.
The first round shot out like a fire hose, the
last part dribbling down her front and onto the
white blouse. For the second round, she was on
all fours. The retching continued long past any
stomach contents.

Terry reached into his suit pocket and handed her his handkerchief. She wiped her mouth
with it and tried to hand it back.

"No, keep it in case you need it again." If he
got it back, he'd burn it. He didn't deal with
unsavory bodily fluids of any sort.

She got in the front seat and leaned her head
back, closed her eyes and whimpered. Sara
more or less fell over and put her head in his
lap. He started the Pontiac, turned on the

lights, and headed to county road AA. The road was a narrow, two-lane road with no shoulders. Its curves made high speed difficult. The road was well maintained except for an occasional "haha" hill. He couldn't remember how old he was when he learned a "haha" was a low fence in England. The sudden up and down giving one's stomach a feeling of zero gravity was called a driver's haha hill. Every haha that they came to elicited a moan from his semi-conscious passenger and "Sorry." from him. Finally, they arrived at the fish camp.

The Lucky Shamrock Motor Court had a hand-painted "Vacancy" sign hanging from it. In front of the office was an RC vending machine and an ice dispenser. In the window, a poster advertising a fishing tournament that took place over a year ago yellowed. The main building was not only the office but the owners' apartment, too. Behind the building stood four cozy looking stone cabins, each had two doors and four parking places. The light was still on. He parked his car and helped Sara sit upright. Then he went in to register.

The office hadn't changed from the time he first came here over a quarter of a century ago.

The calendar behind the counter still read "gift from Hanson's Garage, your neighborhood mechanic." The postcard rack held pictures of the river in the four seasons and some cartoon ones. Next to the rack was one of those cardboard "pharmacies" with aspirin, seltzer tablet, stomach aids, and caffeine tablets. In the glass case were six kinds of cigarettes, eight types of candy bars, lifesavers, and assorted chewing gums.

Centered on the counter was a "Magic 8 Ball" and a bell with a sign, "Ring for Service." He rang the bell and picked up the 8 Ball. "Will I find out who shot at me?" The answer, "Reply hazy. Try again."

The old couple who lived there came tottering through the curtain that acted as a door. He had been watching NOVA on PBS, and she had been crocheting by the light of a table lamp with a picture of Jesus with the Sacred Heart on the shade.

Her voice was like crinkled cellophane. "Would you like a room?"

No, I came here for brilliant conversation was what he thought, but replied pleasantly. "Yes, ma'am, I'll need two. One for me and the other for my niece." The credit card logos were so old that they read "Bank of America" and the "Diner's Club." "I'll be paying cash."

The old lady looked out the window and saw a girl half this man's age apparently asleep in the front seat and no luggage. She could smell the whiskey on him. Suspicion crossed the old lady's brow. "That'll be twelve dollars for the rooms plus sixty-four cents for taxes. I'll need to see two types of ID. We're respectable and don't need any spurious Smith staying here." Then she handed him a registration slip. He registered as, "Terence Rodgers and uh, Mary Rodgers."

He handed her his ID and a twenty. She spent way too long examining them before she handed the IDs and change back. He knew he was hungry and knew Sara wouldn't want anything, so he added: "Give me about four of those Paydays." Then he bought one each of the cardboard pharmacy's offerings. "These, Sara, WILL need, tomorrow if not before." he reasoned.

The old lady pointed to the peg board containing keys, "Ike, you take Mr. Rodgers and his niece to rooms two and three." She wanted them in separate cabins. Ike nodded his head. She went back to her crocheting as he grabbed the keys for rooms five and six.

"I'm puttin' you in, 'cabin three.' I can always convince my wife I heard three and nothing else. I figure you'd want to keep a close watch on your niece. Instead of parking in front, there's a path that goes to the well house, lets you park behind the cabin. It's a bit more private, if you're wanting to make sure nobody knows where you are. Not only that," and he gave him a wink, "The connecting door lock won't hold if you jiggle the door knob a few times." Ike walked to cabin three. Terry bought an RC, then drove behind his cabin. Ike was waiting at cabin's doors. Ike handed him both keys and left, whistling "The Naughty Lady of Shady Lane."

CHAPTER

ELEVEN

Terry opened room six and helped Sara through the door. "Bathroom," she said and they hurried in that direction. He took the opportunity to evaluate their situation. The cabin was orientated so that the headlight of any car turning in would light up both rooms if they kept the curtains open and the Venetian blinds closed. If they kept the rooms dark, no passerby would know anyone was there. He decided on obscurity and made sure her drapes were closed. The room was a different matter. A small window was at the far side of the room but no other exit. The closet and bathroom were opposite the bed. He assumed his room would have a similar design. The room itself wasn't bad. The double bed had a nice handmade quilt and a Jenny Lind headboard. The wallpaper had asters on them, and an old dresser stood on the door side of the bed and a night stand on the other. The nightstand next to the bed had two real glasses wrapped in paper sitting next to the table lamp. He sat on the bed and waited. He heard a flush and then the sink running. Sara, or a phantom that resembled her, emerged from the bathroom and lay on the bed and closed her eyes.

"Don't go to sleep until we..." but she was already passed out. He shook her but only got vague mumblings. Up until this moment, this woman had been just a client and a flake case, at that. Now, something in his evaluation of her shifted. He took a moment to really look at her as a person. She was incapacitated and sleeping in her clothes, marred by vomit. Something about her made him look outside of his self-centered destruction.

He thought, "Poor kid! You don't know who you are or who to trust. You sure drew the joker from the deck when you found me. You haven't caught any breaks, have you? You need someone to look after you until we can find out who you are and where you belong. I guess, for now, that someone has to be me." He stopped his musings and spoke aloud in a quiet, evaluative voice, "You are a mess! What am I going to do with you?" He had to do something about her clothes and her condition. He didn't like bodily fluids, but he had a duty to his client. Terry went into the bathroom and got a wet face cloth. He wiped her mouth and chest clean of the vomit or did the best he could. He couldn't let her sleep in vomit stained cloths. There was only one thing for him to do.

He shrugged his shoulders and started to undress her. He removed her shoes first, because that felt safest for him, given the circumstances. She might wake up. She didn't. Next, he unzipped her skirt. He discovered that some modern fashions do not allow for women wearing any underwear. Even unzipped the skirt was tight and her absolute limpness increased the difficulty and his frustration. Sort of like unstuffing a sausage, he thought. After some moving her back and forth, he was able to pull off the garment. He unbuttoned the front of her blouse, sat her up and removed it. She giggled a bit. He laid her back down, pulled a chair over and checked her pulse. Fifty-eight, too slow. Her chest rose and fell. He watched, up, down, up, down. Her breathing was slow and steady. He began counting her breaths.

"Twelve. Good, she looks okay, but I still need to monitor her." He kept watching her breathe for the next several minutes. After awhile it occurred to him that he had stopped counting breaths. Shaking his head at his thoughts, he went to the side of the bed and pulled the blanket over her and locked the outside door of the room.

Her clothes piled on the floor would be the only things she had to wear, tomorrow. He gathered them together and took two hangers from the closet. In her bathroom, he found a tiny soap. Strange images filled his head of a miniature factory staffed by diminutive workers churning out a full line of miniscule products for motels.

He ran a sink full of water and grimaced as he tried to hand wash the blouse and skirt free of smoke, vomit, and spilled drinks. Then, he hung them from the curtain rod in her room hoping that by morning they'd be dry. Finally, he went back to the bathroom and scrubbed his hands under the hot water until they were almost raw.

The night began catching up with him. He had an overnight bag in the car's trunk. He didn't want to risk going outside to get it. Besides, it was buried somewhere in the depths of the Le Mans' trunk. He had to get to his room next. Ike had been right. A few jiggles and the connecting door opened. Terry got undressed and laid his clothes so they'd be smooth.

Then he took a long, hot shower. It gave him time to think. This woman is my client. Somebody slipped her a mickey. I need to keep an eye on her until she wakes up. She has a pleasant smile! He couldn't figure out why that last thought slipped in among the others. He toweled off and should have gone to bed. Instead, he turned on the light and noticed his room was much like Sara's except he had a chair and a low table for luggage. He took his blanket, the luggage table, and chair into her room. He was afraid to leave his helpless client alone.

He took her pulse, again. Sixty-two, much better. He planned to watch over her until morning. He put the table at the foot of her bed and the chair far enough back to where he could prop his feet up. Back in his room, he picked up his soda and candy bars. He would

"stand watch." Wrapping himself in his blanket, he took his first Payday and pulled the
tab on the can of RC. He ate his candy bar and
sipped the soda, slowly, almost mechanically.
Half way through the second Payday, he
fell asleep.

CHAPTER

TWELVE

The next morning, two things woke him up: the brightness coming through the clothes hanging at the rear window where he failed to close the curtains and a low moan from the bed. He watched her wake up, still concerned about what happened to her the previous night.

Sara's mouth felt like cotton. Her head hurt. She would have sworn even her hair and eye lashes hurt. Consciousness was not coming easily. Sara's eyelids fought a noble battle with her will to determine whether they opened or stayed closed. Her eyelids lost the battle. Slowly, they opened just a crack. "Oh, God, I hope I'm dead. I'd hate to feel this bad and still be alive." She finally raised herself up on her elbows. "Where am I and how did I get here?" she wondered. Slowly she tried to look around the room. After a few failed attempts, she was able to get her eyes to focus. She looked at the bright side of the room. She finally understood that her clothes were the strange curtain hanging in front of the sunny window. As if to verify that they were indeed her clothes, she looked beneath the blanket. She pulled the blanket up under her arms to make sure that she was covered up. When her eyes could focus that far, she saw Terry. Her face flushed red. She couldn't figure out why she was in an old motel with this old man and no clothes. She had meant to play games with his ego, but she seemed to be the one who had been compromised. Sara jerked her arm up, pointing beyond her room, 'Out!'

"I'll, uh.. I'll be in the other room. That one, there," he pointed through the open connecting door. "And ah, ah, you can take a shower and get dressed! I'll be in the other room. Like I said. I'll come back, later." He stammered and for some reason continued to point in random directions. Then he wrapped himself in his blanket, hurried to his room and almost slammed their joint door. Her shower seemed to run forever, but either she ran out of hot water or felt that the last of the previous night had been washed away. Terry got dressed while she was showering. He peeked into her room while she was showering and noticed that she had thrown her clothes on the bed and that they were horribly wrinkled. He turned on his lamp and waited for the bulb to get hot. He ran a damp cloth over her outfit; then he ran the clothes over the top of the shade. It helped take out some of the wrinkles. He gathered up the various tablets that he had purchased the night before. He returned her clothes and put the tablets on her dresser. He waited some minutes after the shower stopped to return to her room. He was sure that she'd be dressed, by now.

She had turbaned her hair in a towel and wrapped herself in a bath towel. "You don't wait for a girl to get dressed, do you?" she demanded, the flirtatious playfulness of the previous evening totally gone, and turned her back to him. "Out!" It was the only communication she had for him. He retreated into his room. He made sure that he faced away from her, as well.

He yelled through the door, "I'll wait for you by the car. I brought you something I thought you'd want this morning. I put them on your hotel dresser."

"If you even mention food, I swear, I will take my high heels and beat you to death. No court in the land would convict me." He did not doubt that she meant it.

He explained "It's just aspirin and caffeine tablets. I think someone slipped you something last night. Take them both and you should feel better, eventually. There's some stomach tablets there, too." He realized that she had gone back into the bathroom. He had to get the furniture back into his room. He quietly reentered her room. He grabbed the two pieces and took them back with him. He made sure to keep his eyes off of the mirror, just in case. He shut the connecting door just as she came out of the bathroom.

Back in his room, he tried to rumple the bed to get that "slept in" look and called out, "We need to leave." He called out again, "The car's behind the cabin. We can talk in the car about last night and, ah, well, things." He yelled through the door but she didn't answer. "That sounded lame. What is wrong with you?" and gave himself a forehead thump. The last thought being more of an indictment than a question.

"I'm parked behind the cabin. The car is, I mean" he informed her, then he grabbed the keys and went to the car. "I'll wait for you there. Outside. Behind the cabin." Why am I repeating myself?

Last night he had been too worried about her to notice very much. This morning, he saw the second bullet hole. He went and squatted down to get a better look. Slowly a realization stole upon him. "If they were trying to hit me, the shooter would have aimed more forward. Sara was the intended target. I hope she doesn't notice the bullet hole." Now, he'd have to play bodyguard as well as detective. Playing bodyguard didn't turn out real well the last time he had done it. There was nothing else to do except wait for her by the car. He opened the passenger door and leaned against the side of the car to hide the hole. He hoped he looked nonchalant rather than nervous.

When she came out, she squinted against the light, opening her eyes only enough to make sure she didn't walk into anything. She went to the passenger door that Terry held open for her and got in. She looked straight forward and folded her arms and had a look on her face that let Terry know he had better tread carefully. Her clothes looked rumpled. Her hair was wet. She still looked like death warmed over.

He could sense that she was just waiting for him to say the wrong thing, anything. As they would say in the spy business, she would terminate him with extreme prejudice. Only about a hair's breadth separated him from this woman's wrath, a wrath he couldn't quite understand. Only when she felt a cool, morning breeze against her neck did she notice the gaping hole behind her. "What happened to the window?" with an astonished voice.

"Someone shot at me last night, and, if you hadn't stumbled, I'd be this morning's front page obituary." He told her, not wanting to let her know what he surmised about who the intended target was. Her astonishment momentarily superseded her anger.

He got in the car and drove it to the office where Ike was sweeping the front porch and gave him the room keys. "Thanks, Ike, my daughter and I had a good night's rest. You take care, now."

Ike gave him a wink. "I thought she was your niece. You are both old enough to know to bring a change of clothes, next time." He went back to his sweeping but started singing "One mint julep was the start of it all."

Sara had her head leaned back and her eyes were closed. As they pulled away she finally spoke. Her voice had a quality he couldn't identify when she said, "I don't remember much about last night and nothing after the last gin and tonic. Tell me everything, and I do mean everything that happened."

As he turned on to AA, he recounted the evening. He made certain to watch the road. "You were there when I arrived. We played the part of a lecherous boss and flirty secretary."

"Office manager!" she corrected him.

He couldn't understand why she would get so hung up on a cover story. Still, if it was that important to her..."Okay, office manager. We danced, had a few drinks and then you went to the ladies' room. You said you found out something and then started acting strange. I was going to take you to a doctor; a fight broke out. I took you to the car. Someone took a pot shot at me. I brought you to the motel. Helped you to bed. You passed out. I had to undress you. I took your clothes and washed them. By the way, 'You're welcome for the laundry service.'" He hoped she picked up on his sarcasm. She didn't. "Then I stayed awake all night making sure you were safe." The story was mostly true and good enough. He liked the part he put in about being the valiant hero who stood as a guardian angel over her, all night long.

Now, she had the awkward questions, "So you didn't...I mean, we didn't. That is..."

Terry interrupted her and replied in a voice that dripped of indignation and disbelief, "You're my client. I have professional ethics."

But something about you sure made them hard to use, he mentally added.

"It's my responsibility to protect you. Besides, I have never had to get a woman drunk to
have her sleep with me. You are young enough
to be my daughter, almost a granddaughter. I
have no delusions that you would find me
attractive. I'll drop you home and take the car
to a body shop a friend has." He started to get
a Payday out of his pocket; then he saw her
chewing a couple of the Pepto-Bismol tablets.
He put it back. He wasn't sure whether or not
her high heel threat was real any more, but the
way this morning was going he wasn't taking
any chances. Neither one of them spoke on the
way back to town.

CHAPTER

THIRTEEN

After dropping her off at her apartment, he went to the industrial part of town where the auto specialty shops operated. Auto Excellence was run by Doug, an old army buddy. After a walk around Doug looked at him and said, "Terry, the good news is that you don't have to worry about the labor to remove the rear window because there isn't one there. Really, besides the window and that 30.06 bullet hole in the rear quarter does it need anything else?"

He knew the answer would be "No." because his friend knew he wasn't going to charge Terry except for parts. Terry suffered from "EWS: empty wallet syndrome." so Terry always had to do everything on the cheap, but he was a good guy.

Terry got out his wallet, that action surprised Doug and gave him his last hundred. Another surprise awaited Doug. Terry smiled at him. "Down payment, Doug, fix her up and paint it like it should be."

"Since you're paying this time, what do you want: the cheap $69.99 job or the paint job done right?"

Terry leaned against the fender and patted the hood. The old Rocket did right by me last night. She deserves a reward. "Paint her up right. Oh, and there's a bad wire to the ignition coil. Right now, I've got to call a cab."

The money and change in Terry's modus operandi took Doug by surprise. It took a moment for him to respond. "Ah, don't do that. Take one of my loaners. But this time, fill it with gas before you return it. Last time, you brought one back so low it took me three gallons just to get it to read empty." Doug tossed him the keys to his loaner, a '66 VW beetle." Terry went to his car and opened the trunk. The inside looked like a flea market exploded. In the jumble he found jumper cables, a metal can of oil, "How old is that?" he wondered as a turned it over in his hands. He saw a book.

"I could've sworn I returned that library book." He slipped it under his arm. He continued to the next level. "Ah, here it is" as he pulled out a gym bag, his overnight stash. He checked it out. It contained a change of clothes, razor, those type of things, and a stapler. "How did that get in there." He looked at the shirt. "Oh, yeah, I used it to fix a hole in the shirt pocket."

He went to the VW and out of habit opened the rear. And there was the engine. Like everything in Doug's shop, it was immaculate. Doug laughed as Terry went to the front and put in his bag. "I can't believe you made a rookie mistake like that!" Doug guffawed and slapped him on the back and went back to his shop.

"At least it is transportation," he thought, and added out loud, "Hey, thanks, Doug. I owe you a big one." And drove to his office.

Terry climbed the two flights of stairs and entered his hallway. He noticed a man at his office pushing a manila envelope under the door. The man saw Terry and began running for the stairs at the other end of the hall. That's when Terry realized he had seen this man last night at the Blue Ohio.

He chased after him, shouting, "Hey, you! Stop!" Terry was out of shape and the other guy wasn't, but he almost had the man when he opened the stairwell door. On the stairs, it looked like the guy was going to get away. In desperation, Terry launched himself toward the fleeing figure and used him to break his descent. Terry made it to his feet first and as the other man was straightening up, Terry landed a good, solid blow to his opponent's midsection. Hitting the well-muscled stomach made an impact but not much. The man's breath came out "Umph."

Terry got ready to hit him again; then he felt a fist hit him just below the solar plexus. He folded and fell. Curled on the landing, he heard the man go down the remaining stairs and out the side door. I'll just lie here and try to re-member how to breathe. After a couple of minutes, he uncurled himself, tentatively stood. He made it to semi-erect. He climbed the stairs, one painful step at a time, using the

handrail as a crutch. It took him several minutes to get back to his office.

By the time he got back to his door he was
almost upright and breathing still hurt but only
when he inhaled. He leaned against the door
and turned the knob. He forced himself to be
fully upright. He smiled and opened the door.
Sure enough, there was Sara. She looked good
with only a trace of the night before clinging to
her. He didn't know that she had been doing a
lot of reviewing of her attitude and actions of
the previous night. She thought that maybe
she had misjudged this older man. She had
decided to really try to help him. She was just
hanging up the phone. It appeared that she had
been organizing the late notices from his desk.
She had opened the envelope that had been
hand delivered and was looking at a note and
photo. She had decided to act professionally in
the office, "Mr. Rodgers, this just came for you
and…" She paused for a moment when she saw
him. He was pale and what he thought was a
smile gave the appearance of a toothy grimace.
"What happened to you? Are you hurt?"

"Oh, I'm okay, just a slight disagreement
between" pointing to the envelope," the

delivery boy and me." Each word still hurt and had escaped through clenched teeth. "I'll be in my office. Give me a minute or two and bring that thing in so I can find out what's so important." He shuffled into his office.

When he got to his chair, he allowed himself the luxury of collapsing into it. Sitting in his chair lessened the pain and after a couple of minutes, if he didn't move, he felt okay. About then Sara came in with a cup of coffee, a stack of messages, the package, and had the morning newspaper tucked under her arm. He took the mug in both hands, held it near his lips, and inhaled the aroma, "Ambrosia." Then he looked at Sara, "You're a God send." She didn't know if he meant it or it was just the caffeine depletion talking.

In the reception area, the phone started ringing. "The phone has been ringing all morning. If this keeps up, I'm going to demand a raise or hire some help." She smiled and held up a stack of messages. "I've arranged them into three categories." and punctuated each group by slapping them down on the desk. "Crackpots," the biggest pile, "Complainers," the next larger pile, "and Potential Clients."

The third pile was small, but to him, impressive. That pile represented more potential clients than he had cross his desk in a month. The phone stopped ringing and a few moments later, picked up the habit, again.

He leafed through some of the crackpots. "Hey, man, you're my role model." A couple farther down the pile. "Does she have a sister?" "Sign me up for detective school."

"Apparently crazy people also have phones," he concluded.

The complainers were no less weird. "Pervert," "Degenerate," "Someone ought to run you out of town. "Stranger and stranger said Alice" came to his mind.

The potential clients were mundane. "I need you to do work for me; please call me at 555-9338" "I'm in a middle of a divorce and need a good PI." read the second. He put the rest of the notes down.

"Sara, what's going on?" Both of them ignored the ringing phone.

She tossed him the paper. "Section B, page 4, Local News." Terry turned and saw a quarter page paid ad. In it was a picture of him holding up Sara. Her face was turned, hiding her identity, but there was no mistaking his. He read the ad for clues: "Confidential Investigations only employee, Private detective T. Rodgers enjoys a night out with a date. Apparently, he likes them young and needs them drunk. Is this the type of man you want heading your investigations?" "They say there's no such thing as bad publicity. But this picture and those shots last night, someone has painted a target on my back or Sara's! Whoever did this had to have a contact at the newspaper to get it in the morning edition"

He knew trying to get anything out of anybody at the paper was hopeless. He turned his attention to the envelope.

He reopened the envelope and poured the contents on his desk: two negatives and another photo of him taking Sara out of the Blue Ohio. In this picture, her face was clearly visible. He took this to mean that he and not Sara was the target of the night. He had to rethink the rifle shots. Maybe, they were for him, after all. The last item fell on the desk: a matchbook from the bar taped to another typed note. "Reputations are delicate things. I will enjoy watching yours go up in smoke." He took another look at the photo. Something didn't look quite right. In his top drawer was a magnifying glass which he used to examine the picture. In the picture, he and Sara were leaving. Almost everyone else focused on watching the fight, everyone but one well-muscled man. "Yes, there he is!" He spun the picture around so Sara could see. "See! Right there." and he stabbed a point on the picture and circled it with his pen.

"What? Who?" she asked, wrinkling her brow as she stared at the circle, hoping to make some sense of Terry's reaction.

Terry handed her the magnifying glass and pointed again with the pen. "That's the mysterious messenger who delivered this packet. He must have had a partner." he proclaimed in a voice that made it sound like he had just found Jimmy Hoffa. He didn't have a name but he now had a permanent record of the face. With a face, he could trace the man. He started to get up, but the pain told him to remain seated. Finding him would have to wait.

He stared at the picture again. "Sara, I haven't gotten very far on your case or Wiresmith's either. I guess I need to really get started, rather than just waiting for someone to give me a clue." He suddenly remembered something. "Wait. You said that waitress Meg had told you where Bandy was. You wouldn't tell me last night. Can you tell me where she is, now?"

Sara shook her head "No." She shrugged and furrowed her eyebrows. "Everything is a bit hazy from the time I left the table until I got back then nothing." She closed her eyes and tried to replay the evening. She had wanted to play games and laugh about his investigating, now she had a vital piece of information, a piece of information that because of her behavior seemed to be lost in the fog of last night. She tried but couldn't remember. She tried recalling any fragment of voice or image. She thought carefully and went through the evening frame by frame. Images and memories started to coalesce. Suddenly, it came back like rummaging through discarded images on a cutting room floor. Dance, drink, restroom. Meg came into focus. Talking about Bandy and, Yes, it was still there. I remember." "I remember!" she said, "Meg told me that Bandy had left to go to a club where she could meet younger men. You know there were some really oolldd guys in there, last night." She smiled and gave him a wink.

The telephone rang. He answered it and the voice on the other end surprised him. It was his client, Mrs. Wiresmith. He didn't know Mrs. Wiresmith knew how to make her own calls.

"Mr. Rodgers, I saw the picture in today's paper. Did you find her? Was that she? Was that my granddaughter? The papers made you sound just awful, but I knew why you were there. You found her, didn't you?"

Terry tried to sound reassuring. "Mrs. Wiresmith, unfortunately, no, that isn't your granddaughter. That was the woman who works with me in my office. Don't lose heart. I do have another lead that might get me a little closer to finding her. When I find her, I'll call you." Mrs. Wiresmith thanked him profusely and hung up.

"Where would the hot place be for Bandy to meet young men?" The last club he'd been to was the "Blue Ohio" and before that was Rte 66, the bar to which he and his buddies went. Back then, cars had round headlights. Old road signs and pictures of the Snap-on calendar girls decorated the interior of that club. The main activities were discussing politics and sports, playing pinball, or later in the evening or deeper in one's cups, solving the world's problems. I remember when Doug and I... That's it Doug does a lot of work for those young professional types." He grabbed the phone and dialed his friend.

"Hey, Doug," he shot his question, "where do the young Turks hang out, nowadays?"

Doug laughed, "If you're using terms like 'young Turks,' you are definitely not in the loop. If memory serves, most the yuppies and preps go to a place out on South Street called 'El Dorado's.' I saw the paper. You looking for a little action? If you are, remember the game has changed since you were young."

Terry returned the compliment, "Yeah, Doug, I hear you. We're both just old roosters now, not young game cocks. Say 'Hi' to Marie, for me. I still don't know why she even puts up with you."

The next thing he did was check the yellow pages. He looked under cocktail lounges. It wasn't there. He tried the newspaper and found it in the "Around the Town" section. El Dorado stayed open six days a week 7 pm to 2 am. He'd have to go out again. More money, Man, I'm glad this goes on Mrs. Wiresmith's account. I just hope mine can hold out until I get reimbursed.

He went to the outer office. He realized that Sara didn't have his address or telephone number. He wrote them out for her and put them in front of her on her desk. "If you need me, I'll be at the library, working on your case. Then tonight I'll be at the 'El Dorado' for the Wiresmith case." She sat up a bit straighter in an increased interest level. He realized that he shouldn't have mentioned the club. For her safety, he didn't want her tagging along. He continued, "And I want you to stay in your apartment, tonight, alone. It's for your own good."

She stood up and came out from behind her desk to look him in the eye. "You can't tell me what to do when I'm not working for you. Where I go in my off time is my personal business." She displayed the attitude of someone who raised themselves and resented anyone telling them what to do. He feared that this aspect of her emerging personality could lead her to serious trouble.

"But you don't work for me. You're a just a client." and opened the door to leave. He thought that statement would end the argument. He was wrong.

She flashed him an "Aha!" smile, "If I'm 'just a client' you can't tell me what to do at any time, because YOU work for me!"

He shook his head. "Now, listen to me, young lady..."

Sara reached into a desk drawer. "Wait a minute; I got something for you. I knew it would come in handy soon."

She pulled out a gift-wrapped box and a card. She had prepared for his paternalistic attitude towards her. "Ta Da," she trumpeted and handed him the gift.

Confusion filled his head, as he opened the gift. It was one of the ugliest ties he had ever seen. "Why?" was all he could manage.

"You'll see." and handed him the card.

He opened the card. The front of the card had a cartoon man wearing a tool belt. He had bandages tied to his fingers and emblazoned across the top "To the world's greatest dad." On the inside, it simply read, "Happy Father's Day." He turned the card so she could see it. "I don't understand. I'm not your father and it's not Father's Day."

"I know that, but with the way you've been acting, I wasn't sure you did."

"Okay, I get your point." He figured that if she wouldn't listen to him, he had better stay close to her for her own safety. "When do you want me to pick you up for El Dorado's?"

"Oh, about seven. We want to get there early." Then, standing on her tip toes, she kissed him on the cheek and whispered in his ear, "Remember, you still owe me one indecent proposal." She watched his cheeks turn red. "Oh, if you're looking for my accident try looking in the Spring." and gave him a light shove towards the door. She had an important telephone call to make.

He stood in the hallway for a moment. What made him uncomfortable about what just happened was it didn't make him uncomfortable. Confused, yes; uncomfortable, no. This is starting to get interesting. He whistled as he went down the hall.

CHAPTER

FOURTEEN

The old library building spoke of learning. The tall arched windows and the columns said that important, enduring things were inside. But that was the old library. The new library had all the character of a cell block. The city had built a massive edifice of concrete blocks with windows around the top. It was as if the architect were afraid that patrons might stage an escape.

The front door had detectors that anyone walking out of the library had to pass through. It scanned for books leaving that hadn't been checked out. Just inside the front doors, the library was guarded by the checkout desk and Emily Yardley, the head librarian, who could have passed as a matron in a 1940s women's prison movie.

When Terry came in, she gave him a smile and a wave. He'd been in so often that he and Emily were friends. He went over to her and returned he book he'd found, Mr. Belvedere. She looked at the card, "Hmmm, overdue by about ten years. If she wore glasses she would have been looking over the tops at them. She said, "I'll call it a found book and take your name off our bad book person list." in a voice she used for seven-year-old children. Then held out her hand. Then she added, "That'll be five dollars."

He reached for his wallet to pay the fine. "Five dollars seems awfully cheap for a ten year fine."

"Oh, I'm not charging you a fine that's why it's a, "found book." I recall, eight years ago you stood there and swore to me, 'I returned that book. I bet you five dollars I returned that book.' Obviously, you hadn't. So five dollars, pretty please."

He laughed "That sure sounds like something I'd have said." and handed her a ten. "Inflation" was all he said.

She didn't have to ask him if he needed help. He did a lot of research here. Metropolitan telephone books, Thomas Registry, Who's Who, and microfilm of major newspapers were at his disposal. He went into the microfilm area and got the Kansas City Star from two to ten years ago, took them to the readers, and threaded the first spool on. She had said to look in the Spring. March through May. A sudden realization came to him. How did she know when to look if she has amnesia? Why did it take me so long to pick up on her statement.? His psyche felt that familiar tug he got when he was being played. Played or not, he had work to do. The frames slid past in a dark and pale blue blur. He started in February, then March. Accidents caused by the icy battles between Winter and Spring filled small places in the paper. Very few resulted in fatalities. April, May, each whirling by.

Two years ago yielded nothing. Three years ago was going the same way. The years unwound but revealed nothing. He kept at it until the tenth year started unfolding. February, the usual. March, first week, nothing, second week, few accidents and death.

March 15, "No nothing" He was scanning so fast that he almost missed it, "accident… alcohol…and there it was, the short article.

"A prominent Kansas City businessman was killed in a traffic accident, last night. Samuel Dayton was traveling north bound on 435 when a Datsun driving the wrong way hit his station wagon head-on. His wife, Anna, son, Jonah, and daughter, Sarah were taken to Mt. Sinai. Charles Haggerty, the driver of the other car, was charged with DUI. Other charges are expected to be filed."

He slowly scanned the next couple of days

Blah. blah, blah. Ah, here it is.

"The wife and son of Samuel Dayton passed away due to injuries they received in a recent automobile accident. His daughter, Sarah, remains in a coma."

It took scanning six months to find the final article: "…heiress…after six weeks in a coma… possible permanent brain injury…3.7 million dollar settlement…no admission of guilt on the driver's part."

"There it was. Sarah's family killed by a drunk driver and she's worth millions."

The coincidence of the alias and her name being the same bothered him. He thought he'd find an answer, but the answer raised more questions.

A good detective knows how to research. Terry took his pad and went to the Readers' Guide to Periodical Literature. Whatever he might have known about amnesia he had forgotten. He looked under "amnesia." The entries were legion. He wrote the magazine names and the key words. Two hours later, he had amassed a great deal of information on "fugue states." The medical aspects of the information lay well outside his expertise. "Now is the time to go see Doc Hunt. Maybe he can put all of this together for me."

Before he left the library, a question kept returning to him. Bill had said that Wiresmith didn't know narcissus from that other plant, ziggie digus venomous, or something like that. He looked in several botanical books until he found it--Zigadenus venenosus, also called

Meadow Death-Camas, often confused with wild onion.

The reading proved interesting. One inter-esting point he took with him: "No known antidote." Bill could have saved him a lot of time if he had used the common name instead of its scientific one. Bill may have been just a gardener, but he was an expert who knew his plants by all of their names.

As he left the library, Emily grinned and used the ten dollars to wave good-bye. Terry chuck-led and waved back. He decided to call on his old mentor, Doctor Joseph Hunt and pointed the VW in that direction.

Doc Hunt lived in one of the houses in the historic district. The house stood up off the ground so high that a short man could walk under it, upright. It stood a full two and a half stories high. It was the flagship home of the neighborhood. Gingerbread decorated the porch. Most of the houses like his were white and stripped of all the elaborate decorative woodwork. His house was yellow with pump-kin toned highlights, and red trim. Some people thought that it was gaudy and showed poor taste. Others called it "garish." He delighted in pointing out that he had experts come and find the original colors of the house. They had told him that only people who couldn't afford to paint their Victorian houses correctly painted them white. His office was in the home's original parlor. He retired from active practice but kept his office available for old patients. That was his explanation, but the real reason was that it gave him a place to hide from his wife's to-do list and smoke his pipe. Doc sat in his luxurious, tucked leather chair. Across from him, in a much less comfortable chair sat Terry. Doc found that an uncomfortable chair encouraged shorter consultations. For longer ones, he had a sofa that matched his office chair.

Terry visited Doc from time to time. He was his mentor. Originally, Doc had been a psychiatrist, but at some point in his career had decided that being a family doctor was more rewarding. He still dabbled in medicine from time to time. He attended conferences and took just enough continuing education credits to keep his license. He had helped Terry survive his meltdown in sixty-five. Doc and Father Peterson had been by his side. Doc was the one that insisted Terry try to write articles related to his work. He had hoped it would help Terry realize that, in spite of what he saw as a personal failing, he was highly skilled and valuable to his professional community.

Now, Terry needed him to clarify the situation with Sarah.

Doc Hunt leaned back in his chair and blew three smoke rings. He stared at a point where the wall met the ceiling. Doc began to explain what might have happened to Sarah. "The brain damage, assuming there was, coupled with the guilt over being the sole survivor can be conducive to a fugue state. These fugues can last a few hours or several weeks depending on the cause of the original altered state and the incident that triggered the current episode."

"But, Doc, what about the name thing."

"The young lady could have been brought partially out of her fugue by the similarities in her location and her name. What was her name, again?"

Terry pretended he didn't remember and pulled his notepad from his jacket pocket. "Let's see. Ah, here, it's Sarah Toni Dayton."

"She told you she became aware at Saratoga and Dayton Avenues. That makes sense. As I suspected, the street names woke her from her fugue state to a degree. Without realizing it, you've been calling her by her name all this time which gave her a sense of comfort and stability. Usually keeping a patient calm is key for a full recovery from a dissociative disruption. I have no doubts; she's made progress. Continue as you are and she will recoup her memories in time."

Terry said, "Doc, I think you hit it square on the head. Thanks a lot." He stood up and turned back, "Mind if I use your phone?"

Doc pulled out his favorite pipe and stoked it. "It's in the hallway. Leave a dime." As Terry closed the door, the smell of cherry tobacco filled the room.

CHAPTER

FIFTEEN

Terry dialed Mrs. Wiresmith. Charles answered, "Wiresmith residence."

"Yeah, Charlie, I know. I need to talk to Mrs. Wiresmith right now."

"Madam is not at home. You may call this evening between seven and nine."

Terry didn't know why he had an instant hatred for anything Charles said, "Can't do it. I'll be on the job then. Just give her the message that although I missed her granddaughter last night, I should catch up to her, tonight, at El Dorado's."

Charles repeated the message and added, "very well, sir." Then "Click." Terry thought

"I don't know how he puts so much snobbery into a click." It had been a long day. He looked at his watch. "I have just about enough time to get home, clean up, grab a bite, and pick up Sara." He did make one stop at a ladies' wear shop. He thought about the way she embarrassed him last night with her antics at the Blue Ohio and that card and gift, today. He decided to play a joke on Sarah and maybe make her blush. Turn about is fair play.

He knocked on Sarah's door. He had the fern from Bill as a house warming. "Just a minute Terry, almost ready."

A few minutes later he heard the latch turn and the door opened. Terry didn't know what fashion statement she'd be making after last night's outfit.

This evening's dress was a modest one. It looked to be dyed in wine with lighter flowers and below the waist, the skirt section had geometric designs and the fabric flowed whenever she moved. Around the waist, a string belt-shaped the dress. The sleeves were long and poofy and had elastic cuffs at the wrist. The neckline had elastic around it and exposed only half of her clavicle. Her make-up was understated and she wore small hooped earrings. The effect was stunning. All he could manage was an involuntary "WOW." All of the sudden, his joke gift didn't seem like a good idea. She looked at the plant hanging from his hand and waited. He suddenly looked down too, as though it had magically materialized. "Oh, I thought you might like a plant for your apartment."

"Not exactly the gift I had hoped for, but it will do." She set the fern on a table next to the door. She stepped out and locked her door. Putting her arm through his, she said, "Let's go have some fun."

She gave a smirk when she saw her chariot for the evening was a VW Beetle. "Cinderella gets a carriage. I get a white pumpkin." When he opened his car door, she saw a present on the seat and got in on her side. "Ooh, a present. I love presents."

Terry tried to snatch it from her. "It's not really a present. Just something I bought, sort of a joke. I thought that after the gift you gave me this morning that I'd... I'll, uh, actually I should take it back."

He found out that getting a gift back from a woman is not an easy thing to do. She twisted away from him, sat down in the seat, removed the card and pinned the box to her lap with her elbow. The card read "After last night; I thought you might want to keep this with you." She tore open the box and there was a teddy. She held up the flimsy garment and examined it. She folded it up carefully and put it away. Sarah turned slightly towards him, lowered her head a bit and looked at him. The effect wasn't coyness. It wasn't meant to be. The look said, "Explain and make it good!" She wondered if he had been honest about last night's activities. Terry could see a slow smolder of mistrust ready to burst into a flame of rage.

Flailing his arms about, he offered a defense. "After last night and how you were dressed,"

"Or wasn't dressed," she interjected.

He kept talking and except for a deeper crimson appeared not to hear her. "And what happened, or more exactly, what didn't happen, I thought you might want to carry a backup in your purse. You know, so you'd always be prepared for anything." He realized that his last statement only made his case worse and could be taken to imply other activities. "It was a joke. I guess, a joke in really bad taste. I'll take it back. And I am sorry." Sincerity filled every syllable and humiliation showed on his face.

"No, I'll just keep it." she smiled, and she drummed her fingers against the gift box. He wasn't sure why, but he felt that somehow his joke would come back to haunt him. Just as he started to back the VW up, she coyly turned her eyes toward him and mused, "Besides, I might need it real soon." She watched the red creep up his neck until he looked like an inverted thermometer. "I seem to make you blush easily." Then she tapped him on the end of his nose. He put the car in gear and drove to the El Dorado without saying anything.

The El Dorado was across from one of the city's public parking lots. The after seven pm free parking made it a prime location. The club operated out of a refurbished warehouse, down near the river part of town. A small, professionally lettered sign hung above the door which was guarded by a steroid created bull of a man. The man stood with his arms crossed, reminding Terry of a Harem eunuch he had seen in his Boys' Picture Book of World Marvels. The only acknowledgment they received from him was a grunt as they passed. He reattached the chain after they entered. From seven to eight, only fifty-two people were allowed inside. The inside was lit with multi-colored lights and one of those disco balls.

A bank of lights moved up and down and spun around, creating an almost nauseating psychedelic effect. At the front of the dance floor on a dais was an emcee and a gigantic board behind him. On the table next to it sat two oversized decks of playing cards. Looking around at the customers, he realized how young they seemed. He felt like a chaperon at a high school sock hop. Sarah blended in with the group with ease. These people came from her social age group. With these people is where she belongs was his assessment. She may have been engulfed by the masses, but she stood out in his mind.

The Emcee cued the house lights and pointed to a group of waiters and waitresses who began handing out a playing card to each patron. Each card had one of those little clips that allowed you to wear it like a name tag. He got the ten of spades. "Okay, for you first timers, here's how we play "Lovers' Poker" at the El Dorado. Each of you has a card. Men have black, the women, red. The chart tells you your match. Here," the emcee pointed at two cards pulled out of the decks. "The four of spades matches the nine of diamonds. They would be a quick couple. You have fifteen minutes find your match and get to know each other. The first time, the ladies come up and draw from the men's pile to find their dates. On the second try, the men draw and then, for the last time, the ladies draw again. Then we mix it up. When the time is up you can either stay with the third date or go back to the one you came with. After that, we draw a card and the winner gets free drinks for the night." A cheer went up.

"Shuffle the cards. Let's play Lovers' Poker." A couple of hostesses arranged the cards.

The ten of spades matched the three of diamonds. After about five minutes of searching, they found each other. The three of diamonds was an Econ Ph.D. candidate, enthralled by the current economic battle. Economics had always bored him, Three of Diamonds, Shirley, talked about her dissertation on "Hayek vs. Keynes: Predictors of Stock Market Fluctuations. He nodded his head from time to time but kept his eye on Sarah who was talking to a tall, tanned, blonde guy.

"He didn't get a tan like that doing honest work." was his evaluation of the man.

"Alright, everyone, it's time to change." Everyone went up and got a new card. Ten of spade had drawn the Queen of Diamonds. He looked around to find her. She saw him at the same time. She was thirty-ish, dressed conservatively. Her dark hair had highlights and her necklace was designed to draw a man's attention to areas below her chin.

"Obviously, she is someone who would enjoy a mature conversation," he surmised. They started walking towards each other.

When they were about five feet from each other Sarah appeared out of nowhere and intercepted the Queen of Diamonds. Sarah pointed to Terry and whispered something to the woman. Sarah walked towards him and the woman walked away. He noticed that her card was the Queen of Hearts.

"What did you tell her about me?"

"I told her you were gay and only came here to troll for guys. Besides, you're supposed to be here on the Wiresmith case and not looking for a date. Me, I have to find the five of clubs. He might be the man of my dreams or maybe just a whimsy." She gave him a "toodles" wave with her fingers. She turned on her heels and disappeared into the crowd.

Terry still had about twelve minutes left. He went to the bar. The new bar was totally devoid of personality. It glistened with newness. A high tech surface with no character guaranteed a quick clean-up. Terry felt that all bars should have personality. The bartender whose name really was "Joe" came up. He looked about sixteen to Terry but was twenty-eight. The only odd thing about him was the delicate crucifix he wore. The short chain on it almost made it a choker. "Hey don't feel too bad." Joe tried to console him. "A lot of women here focus on the young guys. They can't appreciate a true classic."

"You need to work on your people skills. Comparing me to an antique car doesn't help." Terry decided to try to get some information from Joe. "Yeah, I can tell.," then ordered, "Give me a Tequila Sunrise."

Tact may not have been Joe's forte, but he could make a Tequila Sunrise seem to appear almost magically. "Joe, this 'Lovers' Poker' is an interesting game. I've never heard of it before. What is it?"

Joe enjoyed having someone who listened to him for a change. "Yeah, it's our trade mark. One of our regulars invented it, Bandy. She sure was fun to have around."

Rodger's noticed the past tense. "Was fun? What did she do? Move?"

"Not sure. I know she used to live over on Sixth Street. I think she still might. She stopped coming by about a month or so ago. The last time she was in I commented on her necklace. She took it off and put it in my hand. 'Keep it.' she said, 'Whenever you wear it, remember me.' That's just the type of thing she was always doing. Then she left. Best gift I ever got, a real babe catcher. They all ask about it. I kinda miss Bandy."

Terry knew bartenders often had women slip them their names and phone numbers. He noticed his shirt pocket had several such numbers and doubted his sincerity.

He tried to get more information. "Since you don't know how I can contact her, do you have any idea where she worked?"

"Yeah, somewhere downtown at an insurance office or maybe it was a lawyer's. I only remember she was a stenographer and didn't like her job. Maybe, she split and left town. Who knows really."

"Change partners." came over the sound system. Terry went looking for his new "soul mate" the ten of hearts. She was medium height, blonde with the hair falling in soft curls. She chewed gum. No, she smacked her gum. Whenever she talked, she twisted her hair. When he tried to engage her in conversation, her comments gave a new and deeper meaning to the word "vacuous." He felt that he had a more meaningful conversation with the fern.

Terry tried several things. First, he asked her about her leopard clutch purse. She corrected him "It's not real leopard. They are too pretty to make into purses. I think it is made from farm-raised polyesters." Next, he fell back to the common "What's your sign?" line. She brightened up. "Oh, I'm a Pisces. That fish, or is it fishes? I can't remember. Like I was saying, fish, which is strange because I don't like swimming. I like fish. Does that make me a cannibal since I eat fish?" At first, he thought it was a gag. Then he realized, as she went on and on, that she was serious. After about five minutes, Terry understood one thing "This is why trapped animals chew their own legs off." Just when he could take even being in the girl's proximity no longer, time ran out and an arm slipped into his. Sarah came to rescue him.

Relief surged through his psyche. He looked at her and out of the side of his mouth said: "Get me out of this decadent Romper Room!"

She smiled at his predicament and let him steer her toward the door. The MC announced "And the winner of free drinks tonight is," involuntarily, he stopped to hear, "The Queen of Diamonds." A cheer went up from the crowd. The spot light found the Queen of Diamonds and followed her as she went to get her prize. She held her card high in the air and ran up screaming and yelling. She acted like she had won a jackpot in Vegas. "Maybe she isn't all that mature, after all." He started for the door, again.

The Queen of Diamonds walked past them on her way to the dais. Momentary surprise showed on her face when she saw Sara arm-in-arm with Terry. Sarah turned to her and said, "I lied."

CHAPTER
SIXTEEN

Outside Terry noticed two men on the sidewalk, walking towards each other. One of them stuck out because he was dressed to blend in with the club set, but he had a camera, an SLR with a zoomable lens. Terry recognized it immediately because it was just liked the one he used. The other man's outfit was non-descript. He could have easily disappeared into any normal crowd. When they met, both men stopped under a street lamp and then took a couple of steps down an alley.

Terry recognized the second man when he stepped into the light, "It's my dance partner from this morning's stairwell."

He was seventy-five percent sure he was right. "And we have some unfinished business. They say that two's company and three's a party and it is Party Time." To Sarah, he said, "Wait here. If things get ugly, get out of here in a hurry." He forgot to give her the keys to the VW and he was gone before she could point out to him that without them she couldn't hurry away to anyplace.

The two men were at the mouth of the alley. The photographer had just handed over a roll of film in exchange for a twenty when Terry got there. Terry came in low and hard and knocked the man off balance. But the man did a reverse roll and got to his feet. The photographer ran shouting "Help! Help! Police!" and disappeared down the block. He was sure that he was witnessing a mugging and wanted to make sure it didn't involve him.

Sarah moved to a location that gave her a better view of what was happening. Before the other man had centered himself, Terry gave him two quick rights just above the nose. His jabs drew first blood. He was about to land a third swing when the man delivered a counter strike. Both men knew street fighting and how to take a punch. They traded a few more blows. Each one ventured to punch the other in the midsection. Terry knew that eventually, his opponent would reflexively lower his hands. The other man's strategy revealed that he knew that secret, too. Terry had the advantage of height in that he was shorter. The other man had two advantages: he was younger and a better fighter. The last blow that the man got in knocked Terry back a couple of steps. When Terry came forward, he stepped on the neck of a broken whiskey bottle. He fell face first on the bricks of the alley way. A limo pulled up. The rear door opened wide and the man got in. By the time Terry had gotten to his knees, the limo was making a right-hand turn at the light. The man and the film was gone.

About the time the tail lights disappeared, Sarah appeared. She helped him to his feet. She noticed the cuts and scrapes on his face, none of them serious.

"Aren't you detectives supposed to carry a gun or a blackjack or something?"

He limped badly as they crossed the road to the parking lot. He explained to her "Saps are illegal, and guns make you feel like doing something stupid. The cops have guns and that suits me just fine. I promised myself a long time ago to leave the gunplay to the professionals." There was no question in her mind that the matter was closed.

  "Okay, I just thought...." and let the rest of the statement just hang there in the air. This man is no Mannix or even a Cannon. She knew he was right, but she was still a little disappointed. Terry was destroying every stereotype of a detective hero that T.V. had taught her. She helped him back to the VW. As she saw him get into the car, she added one more thought; it dealt with his age. "He's not even a Barnaby Jones!" The odd part was she found all of this endearing.

CHAPTER

SEVENTEEN

The night drive refreshed them. It helped Terry recover faster. The stars seemed near in the clear air and the temperature was cool enough to almost make Terry reach for the heater control. Sarah pulled her arms around her chest to keep warm.

"So cold. When I get home, I'm having some hot chocolate." Sarah made the statement more to the weather than to Terry.

"That sounds good, but I think a fire would be nice." and then noticed that VW seemed to be filling with smoke. The smoke smelled of linseed oil. He jerked the VW to the curb and grabbed the fire extinguisher that Doug put in any loaner. He threw open the engine compartment. A bunch of oily rags stuffed around the exhaust manifold had just burst into flames. In a few more minutes the entire car would have been involved. He shot the extinguisher at the rags.

Although the fire went out some of the rags some still smoked. He reached in and using two fingers grabbed at the pieces, burning himself alternately on the hot metal and the smoldering rags.

About that time a police car pulled in back of them. A tall, sandy-haired man got out. He looked to be a good ten or fifteen years younger than Terry. He looked at the VW's engine, then at the smoking remnants of the oily rags lying behind the car. He straightened up and pushed his hat back on his head. License and registration, please." He needed the information if he decided to fill out a report. "You folks were lucky. Good thing you had an extinguisher."

Terry fished around in the glove compartment until he found the car's papers. Sarah tapped her foot on the sidewalk, her arms still folded across her chest. She hummed and looked at an imaginary point in the sky. She gave the impression of a woman perturbed either at the delay or the driver. He noticed the cuts on Terry and noticed the package in the back with a bit of lace sticking out. He looked at Sara, "Miss, is everything okay here?" He handed the information back to Terry, "Sir, would you mind explaining those cuts and scratches on your face to me?"

Before Terry could utter a word, Sarah started talking. "Officer, those are all my fault. I told my boss I was going out and he's such a gentleman." She pointed to Terry. "He told me that I shouldn't go out alone because it's unsafe for a young, single woman and when I didn't agree with him, he insisted that he escort me. He told me that Canaan wasn't the same place that it used to be when he was growing up. A young woman shouldn't be out unaccompanied. People have been known to put things in women's drinks. You know, I think that's actually the first time he referred to me as a woman. Usually, my boss just calls me, kid. Anyway, we came here and I was playing that Lover's Poker and well, he had to play too. When this younger chic made a move on him and I could tell he was uncomfortable. I went to rescue him. We left and were going to the car. He slipped on some broken bottle or another and BOOM, down he went. So you see, it's all my fault. I shouldn't have insisted on going out." Terry had never heard anyone say so much, so fast, in a single breath as his client had just done. Terry noticed that the cop had seen the package but didn't say anything. He was wondering how Sara would have explained that if asked.

The policeman shook his head.

Halfway through her conversation, he had recognized the two as the couple in the paper. "Young lady, you should listen to your boss. There's a lot of crime in this town. And you sir, I'm giving you a break. It seems like you had a little bad luck, tonight. Some mechanics get a bit careless with rags and such. I once found a timing light left on my engine. Kept it. You need me to call a tow truck?"

Terry knew this was no accident. That engine had been spotless and the rags didn't smell of motor oil and "Go-Jo" but of linseed oil. Someone had stuffed the rags around the exhaust while they were in the nightclub. He needed the policeman to leave; so, he kept his thoughts to himself and continued to focus on the officer standing before him. Terry had been trying to look interested, as though the officer was giving him clues to the secret of the Sphinx. The last question caught him off guard. "Huh? Oh, no, I'll call AAA. We'll have to wait here; then we'll get a cab."

The officer turned to go back to his car. "I'll patrol by here a little longer, 'til you're both safely on your way. Protect and serve, you know." Then he gave Terry a wink, "Serve and protect." He reached into his patrol car and grabbed the two-way radio, "This is Officer Barker, clearing the scene." He got in and drove off.

Terry held the door for Sarah to get in the car. Next, he looked up and down the road. He was looking for any signs that they might be followed. If someone were following them, maybe, the patrol car had scared them off. The road appeared to be empty. "Good! No traffic. It might be safe," he assessed the safety of their location. He told Sarah, "I better call Doug and let him know about the car. You stay here where it's safe. I'll be right back." He jogged down to the corner to call Doug from a pay phone. It took him a little while to catch his breath. Marie answered. "Hey, Marie, it's me, Terry. Tell Doug the VW caught fire. It's okay, though. It's on Elm Street, near Lincoln Avenue. Gotta run. I've got a client that I need to get back to." He got out another dime. Hometown Cab promised to send a unit to his location in about fifteen minutes.

As he walked back to the VW, he noticed that the passenger door was open and Sarah was not in sight. He picked up his pace to a slow run and looked from side to side, scanning for any signs of people or cars. He couldn't figure out where she might be. Sarah doesn't realize the danger for her. Where can she be? I didn't hear or see anything. When he got within a few yards of the car, her head came up, and she appeared to be fiddling with her ear. He returned to a walk and then got in his side of the Beetle. "When I didn't see you, I got nervous. I thought maybe something had happened to you." he gasped and added a mental note, "I definitely have to start exercising."

"I dropped an earring," she explained.

Simultaneously, they turned to each other and in unison said, "We need to talk." Terry trying to sound very gallant pointed his hand to her as if granting permission, "You first."

A look filled with worry crossed her face. Her voice was heavy with concern. She took both of his hands in hers. She twisted her torso so she could look him in the eyes. "Terry, I think you ought to go to the police about these death threats you're receiving. I read them in your office. You were shot at and, now, they tried to burn you alive. One day, you're going to run out of luck."

He moved his hands. He held her right hand in his left and his other hand over it. "I was going to say the same thing to you. I looked at where the bullet hit. I think they were aiming to hit you. Then there's the timing. I've been driving around all day in a car no one knew. The only way to identify it was when I went to pick you up, unless..." A thought came to him when he remembered his conversation with Charles. Why would the butler have anything to do with this? But I did tell him where I'd be and when. The butler did it? Nah, too cliché.

He turned his attention to Sarah. "They had to see us together. Any idea why someone would want to harm you?" The absurdity of asking such a question to an amnesiac did not escape him.

Sarah chewed on her bottom lip a moment then opened her mouth, started to say something, then cut any word short. She locked her lips together, shook her head and finally said "No. I don't think I need the police. You will just have to be my personal bodyguard." She didn't know why Terry winced when she mentioned, "bodyguard."

"Still no cab!" Terry decided to tell her everything he knew: The accident, and deaths, the court awarding her all that money. Finally, he added, "...and your name really is 'Sarah Dayton.' But it's Sarah with an, 'h.'"

She received the news stoically and at the last piece of information, she sucked her lips over her teeth, like a small child caught in a lie, then added, "I know."

"What! How long have you KNOWN?"

"Since I woke up this morning in the Lucky Shamrock motel. You see, this time it was different. Normally, when I have one of these spells, they last about three or four days, but I don't remember what I did. When I 'came to' this time, I remembered everything. Except whatever happened after that last drink, including how much you seemed to need help. And I was having fun being your office man-ager. I wanted to keep doing it. You're not mad at me, are you?" She steeled herself for one of his explosive responses.

Two days ago his reaction would have been atomic, but he had been thinking about what Bill told him, what he told Bill, and about a certain stupid fern. "Hey, I had some fun, too. It was nice to have coffee and a smile in the office for a change. Do you have any idea what caused you to black out?" He still hadn't let go of her hand.

Sarah, having steeled herself for an outburst, felt let down by Terry's reaction. She told him "All I remember was KCMO ran a story about the accident. The man who caused it commit-ted suicide and the note said he couldn't live with the guilt any more. His wife, on the air, said that I was just after the money and her husband's death was my fault. Then the station replayed the accident using pictures the police had. Even though they were black and white, it was my family." Tears were coming down her cheeks and gentle sobbing noised arose from her. "The next thing I knew, I was standing on that corner." He handed her his handkerchief. She dabbed her eyes and blew her nose and offered it back to him.

"No, no, you might need it again." He was very sympathetic but he still did not like bodily fluids.

Suddenly he felt uncomfortable, or perhaps just a bit foolish. He gently removed his hand from hers and used them to gesture as he looked around. "And when the cab gets here we are going straight to your apartment. I'm spending the night."

A hint of a wicked smile touched the corners of her mouth. "Oh, my! What a roguish protector I have. I hope my virtue will be intact in the morning and me with a new teddy that you just happened to give me."

Memories from the Lucky Shamrock Motor Court briefly filled his mind. Terry could feel himself turn red, again. "Why do you do things like that to me?"

She smiled a full wicked grin. "Because you are so cute when you're embarrassed. She took her index finger and tapped him on the end of his nose. She thought about her intent when she went to the Blue Ohio. It was still a game with her, but the game had changed and the goal different. The problem was that she didn't know what the purpose or goal of the game was. In the mirror, he saw lights and prayed they belonged to the cab. As the vehicle approached, he could see the light on the top indicating the cab was available. Almost immediately behind him was a tow truck.

The cabbie opened the doors for them. Sarah insisted on getting her present from the VW while Terry secured the Bug. He got his bag out from the trunk and handed the keys to the tow truck driver and told him to deliver it to Doug's. He made sure that he had the address.

When he got in the cab, Sarah looked at the satchel, "You look pretty prepared. An overnight kit?"

"I always carry one. As a detective, one has to try to anticipate every possible scenario and outcome." He knew that he sounded pompous. He, also, knew that he was telling her the truth.

The cabbie was tired of waiting. "Where you two want to go." Sarah gave him the address to her apartment. She wasn't sure if it was because she needed Terry to protect her or if she wanted to protect him.

On the way to her apartment, they made what to the outsider seemed to be idle conversation. They turned their heads towards each other and talked about dances and the El Dorado and about maybe going picnicking at the river by the "Shamrock Inn." The coded conversation carried no interest for the cabbie. Terry would from time to time turn his head a bit more. At one point, he indicated a street. "The Wiresmith estate is down that road and where it tees you turn left."

Sarah made a mental note of its location. This conversation permitted him to point and turn. He noticed that they were being followed. He had to wait until the car behind passed under street lights. It was a dark blue Buick. About five blocks from Sarah's apartment, it got stuck at a red light where a police car sat.

Terry gave a sigh of relief and continued their inane conversation. They were down to discussing office furniture by the time they got to Sarah's. He didn't want to tell her about the Buick that he thought might be following them ever since the taxi turned onto Lincoln Avenue.

CHAPTER

EIGHTEEN

When they got to her apartment, he insisted on going in first. She decided to let him play "knight in shining armor." He turned on the lights and inspected each room. She knew he was worried about her, almost as much as she was about him. She still thought that he was most probably the target.

The living room first, then the coat closet. Next the bedroom. He opened its closet "Where did she get all these clothes!" came to mind and made him pause for a second or two. Then he checked the bathroom which was between the living room and the kitchen. Finally, he closed all the curtains. "It's safe for you to come in," he declared.

"Wanna bet!" she countered and walked in holding her teddy in front of her. She put it back in the box and set her gift down on the coffee table. She wanted to make sure that he had to look at the box. "Sit down. I'll put some coffee on. I think I might have a stale doughnut or two in here."

He sat on the sofa, pondering over how he could keep her safe and investigate at the same time. No one has bothered her apartment. Maybe whoever it might be, doesn't know where either of us live. He was hoping that he could lay out a plan to her that, if she followed, would keep her safe. He doubted it would do any good. She seemed impervious to good advice. No plan appeared but a couple of germs of ideas started to grow. Their growth was interrupted by Sarah bringing out a tray of coffee and some of those gourmet cookies supermarkets sold.

While they drank coffee and had the cookies. "It just doesn't make sense. This guy has missed twice and those oily rags, strictly amateur night stuff. I can't see either one of us being a target. You don't know anyone in town. Come to think of it; you didn't even know what town you were in. No associates, no history, no real motive."

"What about you? You have a history in this city and have probably made an enemy or two." Her point seemed to be well made.

"No motive. For the last fifteen or twenty years, I have been going through the motions and that's it. Just sleep walking through life. The last three years, I wasn't even doing that. If anyone wanted me to suffer, they'd leave me in my current position, instead of putting me out of my misery. Frankly, I haven't done anything in the last couple of years that could ruffle anyone's feathers. Take my last case: a father wanted me to check out her boyfriend. The kid had the most boring, squeaky clean life one can imagine." Inside his head, other thoughts were disturbing him. Why am I running on like this? You may be this pathetic, but why tell her?" He knew that he was trying to dig a moat to go with the wall he built when he dealt with people. "I think we better get to bed so we can tackle this in the morning." He stammered a bit. "Ah, ah, I mean you had better go to bed and I'll sleep out here."

"Okay, I'll go first" was all she said. She went and got the package with the teddy. She held it in front of her and drummed the box with her fingers. "I think I'll take my shower then slip into something more comfortable." and gave him a wink and tossed the teddy on her bed.

After she finished her shower, she came out in her heavy, terry cloth robe. Her hair bound up in a towel around her head. She entered her bedroom and started to close it. "Keep your bedroom door open so I can keep an eye on you," he called after her.

She stuck her head back out of the door. "Voyeur!," And tossed him a blanket. Then with a quick toss of her head and a backward kick of her foot, like the end of a burlesque routine, she shut the door.

He lay down on the almost long enough sofa. His head rested on his arms that were folded on the throw pillow; his feet sat on the arm of his makeshift bed. He looked up at the ceiling and thought. Sleep wouldn't come. Every creak and imagined noise set every nerve of his on full alert. Not since back in sixty-five had he felt like this, worried and protective. Not since Janice, had a woman brought up these emotions at the same time. Maybe, it was acting as body guard. The light from the clock on the kitchen counter kept dropping minutes like a Chinese torture. Even the hours entered the progression. Eleven, twelve, one, one oh eight. Her bedroom door opened. He sat up. He had been awake before but trying to sleep. Now he was fully awake. He had relegated sleep and unnecessary and undesired. Sarah came out of her room. She was wearing what he could only guess was a modest nightgown and that terry cloth robe. She sat down beside him. "I can't sleep. Could we watch some late night TV or something? I don't want to keep you from getting sleep."

He looked at her, "I wasn't sleeping. I was watching out for you." He changed the topic. "Got any popcorn?"

She shook her head "No," and added "You didn't get any sleep last night, watching me, now again, tonight. You are going to kill yourself that way."

Terry shrugged, "Sleep deprivation comes with the job, sometimes." Watching T.V. sounded like a good late night activity. "No popcorn, huh? I guess we'll just have to watch TV without it." He got up and tuned the TV to one of those UHF stations. The late night movie was "Easy Living," one of those 1930s screwball comedies where the girl was mistakenly identified as a rich man's mistress. The station seemed to interrupt the show every seven minutes with eight or nine minutes of commercials. Somehow or another, his left arm found its way around her shoulder. She was holding his left hand and leaned her head against his chest. It felt good. By the time the movie had unraveled the confusion, they were both fast asleep.

Terry had strange dreams. The Queen of Spades was running around saying, "Off with her head." The Knave of Diamonds, for that's what they called the Jack in his dream, was in the garden shooting at everyone with a cork gun. Then the Jack morphed into an Indian with a flaming arrow. Terry flew overhead in a World War I Nieuport biplane with no machine guns. All he could do was shout at the knave / Indian "Bang! Bang!" Then the Queen of

Spades reappeared, but she was calling herself the Queen of Clubs.

Behind her back, she carried a huge cartoon hatchet. In a sweet voice, she was calling, "Here, kitty, kitty. You need to stop hiding and get some milk." He rose to consciousness for a moment. Then came the dream replay of, "the Incident."

Once again he was in his thirties. He had gotten a tip on the bank robber that had shot a policeman. He was determined to bring him in for the reward and the recovery fee. He could have called the police, but he'd lose out financially, and, besides, he was every bit the detective that Peter Gunn was. The man was holed up in an abandoned house. Terry saw the action in third person. He watched as he went up the steps of the porch. "Bradley Branford, give yourself up." the dream Terry yelled. Branford fired through the door as his response. Terry returned fire, got off four rounds and then his gun jammed. He thought he hit the robber in the arm.

Branford escaped through the back door. Terry gave chase. In a dream you never get tired. Like running a demented obstacle course, Terry jumped over garbage cans, ducked under clothes lines, and hurdled at least one sleeping dog. Branford managed to make it to a convenience store where he saw a Valiant with the driver's side open and the engine running. He jumped in it and tore out of the parking lot. The small car was t-boned by a speeding '63 Corvette, driven like a demon by the teenager who had just stolen it. Terry didn't know there was an infant in the back seat until it started crying. He ran to try to save the infant, but the baby had died in his arms and Terry was covered with his blood.

The three involved in the accident died at the scene. Everything went black, and all he could hear was the mother's screams and sobs. He woke up with a start. He could just make out the clock on the wall. It read six o'clock. He was sweating in a near panic. He always tried to hide from that dream. He usually hid from it by crawling into a bottle of anything alcoholic. This time he couldn't "I don't know if there's anything to drink in Sarah's place." To help his head get on straight, he focused on the first dream. Maybe it was trying to tell him something.

He carefully got up so as to not disturb Sarah. They had fallen asleep leaning against one another. He laid her down on the sofa. As he covered her up with the blanket, he thought, "This is starting to be a habit." To make sure nothing woke her up, he turned off the TV which was just beginning its broadcast day, according to the announcement. Just below her wall phone was a drawer full of the detritus that all such drawers collect. In it, he found a pad and a pencil. He wrote a note for her. "Go to the office and wait for me there. Do not pass Go. Do not collect $200. I'm serious, only to the office." He planned to break a promise that he had made to himself over twenty years ago.

CHAPTER

NINETEEN

He walked four blocks from the apartment before he dared call a cab. When the cab pulled up, he was in it before it had fully stopped. "McCrary building." he barked at the cabbie.

"Yeah, sure, Mac." the cab driver replied between teeth that were clamped down on a cigar. The street lights were going out, and the commuters and people going to open their shops were the only traffic on the streets.

He didn't have a plan and was still playing "connect the dots" when he got to the building. He had keys in hand. "Wait here." was his command to the cabbie. To get everything done by nine allowed no time for mistakes or false starts. He ran up the steps and was like a dervish in his office. He went to his office safe.

In his hurry, he had to try four times to get the combination right. When the door opened he pulled out a lock box. He unlocked it and took out the three things it held: his thirty-eight, his shoulder holster, and a much smaller model 1908 semi-automatic twenty-five caliber "backup" pistol. He put the box back and closed the safe with a vengeance and spun the dial. He slipped the shoulder holster on, checked the thirty-eight and the twenty-five. Both magazines were empty. The thirty-eight went into his holster, and the twenty-five slipped into his hip pocket. He made sure he locked everything back up and left.

The next place he needed the cabbie to take him was to the Avis car rental at the airport. The cabbie dropped him off and received a generous tip on top of the fare. "Buy your wife some flowers. Tell her you love her."

"Yeah, sure thing, Mac." a smiling cabbie replied. As he drove away, he chuckled to himself, "I ain't even got no wife."

At the Avis counter, Terry insisted on renting a green Dodge. It was a car unlike any vehicle that he drove, and he hoped would offer him a bit of anonymity. Fortunately for him, the company was able to meet his request.

His first stop was a home out on Adams Street. He drove down the street until he saw the sign: "Hank Jarvis Leather Goods: Hand-made excellence."

He drove through the open gates and coasted to a stop. He didn't want to disturb Hank's wife. This had to be a covert visit. Terry knew that Hank would be in the shop. He told Terry that he started his workday at five am, every day. On the door hung a sign "OPEN." The light was on in the old detached garage. Inside, the leatherworker was lacing something. Terry stuck his head in, "Hey, Hank, how's it going?"

A man of seventy-something looked up from his work table. Tooled leather pieces laid together in a confused pile, confused, except to a craftsman like Hank. "Making a fancy saddle bag for a weekend cowboy. What brings you to my part of town and so early? You usually don't get here until afternoon. Come rest of the way in and sit a spell. Get you a cup of coffee." Hank pointed to the always present coffee pot.

Terry stepped into the shop. The rich smell of leather was like incense to his spirit. Normally he would have picked up a scrap and inhaled more deeply.

Hank's workshop made people slow down and appreciate his craftsmanship. In the display cases sat the smaller items: assorted wallets, key rings, and other leather items of unknown use.

On one wall hung a wide variety of handmade belts. On another were hand-tooled purses, holsters, and sheaths.

Behind Hank was a metal grillwork door, recycled from an old elevator. The grillwork allowed people to look into his store room of assorted metal objects used in leather products. The grillwork kept the leather that was in there from mildewing. On the wall opposite Hank were the antique leather items he displayed. If it were old and leather, Hank put it there.

Since Terry didn't get his normal cup of coffee, Hank realized there must be some urgency. Hank repeated, almost paranoid, "Terry, what do you need?"

Terry showed him the small gun. "I'm looking for a thigh holster for this gun. Do you have one that I can give to my secretary?"

"Office manager," he heard Sarah retort in his head.

The old man pushed his chair back, stood up and stretched his shoulders until Terry heard a "crack." The surprise that he felt, seeing Terry with any firearm didn't show on his face.

"Unload it and hand it here. I might have what you need in the back. I haven't had anyone ask for one of those since Jimmy Carter got elected."

Terry removed the magazine and pulled back the slide. A round of ammo leapt from the chamber. "That's why I have the owner check his gun." He would have added, "You should have known better.," but he knew his friend hadn't touched a gun since 1965.

Terry felt chagrinned. Even though the magazines had been empty, he forgot to check the gun itself. It was the type of rookie mistake that cost gun owners their lives.

Hank went to the back room. Terry could hear old file cabinet drawers being pulled open and slammed shut, and Hank muttering to himself, "Not there, nope, that's not it. Oh, here it is, no, that's not it." and finally "Eureka," Hank's telltale comment when he finally found something. He brought out the holster. The elastic bands designed to hold it in place gave it the appearance of a deadly garter. "Just let me fix it up, and she's ready to go." He cut off the old elastic the made up part of the belt that went around the thigh. Next, he went over to his sewing machine and reattached everything to the new elastic. "There you go. To anybody else, it'd be forty-five dollars. For you, let's call it thirty. And he put the holster in a brown bag.

Terry had exactly eighty dollars. One of his bills was a fifty. He handed the fifty to Hank. "Keep the change." Terry's generosity never surprised Hank. The fact that Terry had money did. Hank got out an old, worn out wallet. "I ought to get a new one from over there" pointing to a case, "but I don't think I could afford what I'm asking for it." It was a standing joke that Hank always told. Both of them laughed,

Hank because he always did. Terry because Hank was his friend.

He left Adams Street and headed to the bank. The lobby opened early. The bank was trying "customer friendly hours," one or two days a week. Terry looked at his Timex watch.

"Nine o'clock and I'm still not half way through what I need to do. I hope I have enough in the account." He had calculated what he thought his expenses might be. His account should have a hundred or a hundred and a half. He had gone through a lot of money in the last day or two. This day might cost him two hundred, maybe more, but he knew his account must be getting low.

When Terry entered the bank's lobby, the atmosphere was different. The uniformed security guard came up to him and slapped him on the back. "Night life must be a right life for you. Looking good."

An uncertain smile crossed Terry's face. "Thanks. You know how it can be." He hoped that he sounded like he knew what the guard was talking about. Two of the bank's officers waved at him. The bank advertised itself as "the friendly bank," but normally, he didn't get this recognition. He waved back.

At his favorite window was his favorite teller, Mavis. "Morning, Mavis, I need my business' current account balance and to cash a check."

She winked at him, "You must be planning another night out. If you need a disco date, call me. I love dancing. If my husband and kids say okay, we can make a night of it. Your balance is two thousand eight hundred forty-six dollars and eighteen cents."

Any other morning he would have been flabbergasted and wondered where the extra twenty-seven hundred had come.

Today, he felt that the world had gone mad, but he didn't have time for analysis. He wrote the check for four hundred dollars. As he pushed it through the cage to Mavis, he told her, "Just make the four hundred two fifties and the rest smaller bills."

Mavis counted his money back to him and finished with, "Now, don't you forget your dear Mavis, if you need to go dancing." He ran with the theme, "Now, Mavis, if I took you dancing it would break poor Harry's heart."

He paused and let Mavis think for a moment about her husband. Then he finished, "Anyway, I promised I'd take HIM next time." They both laughed.

Mavis ended the banking transaction with, "You are a scamp! Now you come back real soon, darlin'. NEXT." She gave him a parting wink and a smile.

The morning traffic had picked up. Now, people who were late for work or trying to get the family shopping had done filled the streets. He had his own shopping to do and drove to a sporting goods shop. This shop had an advantage over most others. It had a private shooting range. Once inside the store, he walked deliberately to the gun section. A friendly face belonging to someone his age came up to him, "Yes, sir, may I help you?"

"I need a box of .25 caliber shells and four, no, make that five boxes of .38s and, I need my guns checked out."

The man handed the gun to someone named "Greg" who took it over to a work table. With speed born of expertise, the man took the thirty-eight apart. While Greg cleaned and oiled the gun, he shook his head, muttering about proper gun care. He got to the twenty-five caliber and saw the years of neglect, he glared at Terry as though he were guilty of some type of criminal abuse. "This one needs a new spring," was all he said.

"Replace it, and if you have an extra magazine for it, I'll take that, too." He hoped to redeem himself in the eyes of the gunsmith. It didn't help.

Greg returned the guns to him. "You got you a couple of nice guns, but you need to treat 'em right. That 1908 hasn't been made since 1921, and if you had tried to fire it, the slide would have jammed up everything. No new magazine for it. I could order you one. That'll be $28.13. Pay the cashier."

Terry took the guns and added "I wanted to use your shooting range. I know it's a private one, but I need the practice."

Greg looked at him; then a practiced eye saw the hint of a shoulder holster. "In that case, pay me and add a twenty," he thought about the man in front of him and the condition of his guns, "no, make that thirty." When Terry gave him seventy and told him to keep the change, Greg handed him a box. "It's a gun cleaning kit. You're going to need it." Terry noticed it had all the extras.

When he entered the private range which was technically next door. He bought human silhouettes, instead of the bulls-eye ones they provided. The first box of bullets proved the safest place to be was in front of the target. The only hole in the target hit it right in the appendix. The problem was he had been aiming at the head. His hand didn't want the bullet to hit anyplace fatal. By the time the fourth box was shot up, he was hitting the target three out of six times, sometimes even in a fatal area. He loaded up the twenty-five and shot one magazine just to see if was working correctly. He made sure to clean the guns with the new kit before he left. The next stop was the newspaper morgue.

CHAPTER

TWENTY

The newspaper kept archival papers for researchers. Terry was looking for an obituary. He felt time being squeezed out of his day like water out of a rag. He found the obituary:

Harold Amadeus Wiresmith, industrialist and philanthropist...died today...survivors...wife Sandra McClain Wiresmith and a granddaughter, Amanda Jane Setrap...

McClain, not Setrap. She had said all the women in her family. Only she's a McClain, not a Setrap.

He didn't have all the pieces, but they were falling into place. He thought about how the book had said that the bulb of Meadow Death-Camas looked like onions and what Bill had said. Those hairs on the back of his neck were giving him some really bad vibes. Apprehension started to creep into the fringes of his mind. He knew he had to talk with Sarah and work out a plan for her ultimate safety.

When he got to the building, he parked the Dodge across the street instead of in the parking lot. He didn't want to make it easy for someone to connect him with the car. He made sure to lock it. He looked around and saw that no one was following him or watching him.

Upstairs more activity was going on. The offices next to his seemed to have new occupants, or at least, some remodeling going on. That office had stood empty for six months or more. In his office he could hear, "Yes sir, I'll be happy to have him call you, but our calendar is a bit full."

He entered the office, and an extremely frustrated Sarah was on the phone. Sarah saw him walk in.

Finally, she had someone at whom she could yell. "That's it! If this doesn't stop by noon,

I'm hiring a temp! The paper did it to us, AGAIN. LOOK!"

She had turned the paper to the page 5 on the local news section. The picture in the quarter page ad was of him in the El Dorado. He was with the vacuous girl whose back was to the camera. Behind him was the banner "Love Poker Tonight: Get Lucky in Love." The printing stated "He's three months behind on his rent. He overdrew his bank account twice last month. He had to fire his secretary. But he has no trouble dancing disco. Would you trust this man, Terence Rodgers, to investigate a problem for you?"

Sarah was on a roll. "I'm going through notepads like crazy. There are two men in your office who insists you need to see them, not them see you. I told them that you'd be very late, but one of them, I'd say the man in charge, said he'd wait. Let me know, next time if you are making appointments. I need to know about it if I am going to manage your office" She pushed her hair back as a sign of her mounting frustration.

Terry noticed that she seemed to be taking her cover very seriously. He wondered why she was still here. He had found out what she wanted to know. She didn't need his services any longer. "It won't happen again." He didn't know who wanted to see him, but he didn't want her to know that. He slipped his hands into his sports coat pockets and closed his right hand around the twenty-five and walked into the inner office. One thing he noticed was a new, small refrigerator against the wall. The other thing was an executive type was sitting behind his desk. He recognized him as the man who helped him when his car wouldn't start. The man standing at his side was the "Delivery Boy."

The seated man began to speak. "Mr. Rodgers, I am Saul Overstreet, perhaps you remember me." A statement, not a question. Terry nodded his head and tightened his grip on the pistol as he slipped the safety to "off."

"I was confused when I got into your office. It had style. I thought I might have misjudged you. I thought 'He's a man with awareness. Perhaps, I should have just come and talked with him.' Then when I came in here." His arms made a sweeping motion around the office. "You didn't disappoint. This IS the office of a second-rate shamus who makes his living peeking through keyholes and playing very loose with the truth, the sort of man whose mind doesn't think, but only reacts. I came here to tell you that I decided to destroy you. But now, I see you aren't worth my trouble or the minimal effort it would take. The reception area just doesn't fit." Overstreet added just as an observation.

Terry looked him squarely in the eye. "So you're they one who tried to shoot me and torch my car, or more exactly, your silent partner standing beside you." He kept his eye on the "delivery boy." He had the idea that that was the possible point of trouble.

"Mr. Rodgers." It was Mr. Overstreet turn to be confused. "I have no idea of what you speak. You told Mr. Ford that I was a gangster, which I am not. That misinformation hurt someone in my family. I may know some people in organized crime. In my business, I might, I said 'might,' have to deal with them, but I am a legitimate union official. That report caused problems for my nephew. I hired Mr. Camford, a reputable private investigator to research you and get pictures that I could legitimately use to cause you grief. I made very sure that no one but you would be hurt by the publicity. I am not a blackmailer or a thug. I came here so you would know who is responsible for all the grief that has fallen on your business and to let you know it is over. My nephew and his girlfriend got married. The matter is ended. Good day." Then he and Camford left.

Terry allowed himself the luxury of exhaling. He put the safety back on. He found a small bag for the holster and gun. He put them in his middle desk drawer. If they aren't the perpetrators, then Sarah is still in danger. I have to make sure Sarah is protected. He just wasn't sure how to tell her. He started laughing. It helped relieve his tension, and he thought about Mr. Overstreet's strategy and how it had backfired. I have more people wanting my services now than in a long time. I wonder what he'd think if he found out that his plan turned into one of the best advertisement campaigns.

The day was not going how he had planned. Whether that was good or bad, only time would tell. He looked at his watch, 11:30. He went out to the outer office. Sarah was on hold with another caller. He started to say something and she held up one finger to shush him, "Just a minute."

"...yes, yes, that's right. One thirty. Yes, that will be fine." Then she hung up. "The temp, Anita, will be here this afternoon."

"Fine," he had given up all hope of knowing what was going on in his own office. "What say we go to the Clark's Diner and grab some lunch? My treat. When we get back, I have something to give you."

"Lunch sounds good, and after last night's teddy, I can't wait to see what you have for me this afternoon." Sarah enjoyed having something meaningful to do, even if it was only helping a third-rate detective agency from going under. And the detective, Terry, definitely needed someone to give him a sense of direction. He, certainly, wouldn't have been able to handle any real business like they had been getting recently. On the way out, she knocked on Artemis Franklin's door. When he answered, she said, "Mr. Franklin, I would like for you to take care of that matter while we are out of the office for lunch." Terry assumed the janitor had missed some cleaning in his office.

CHAPTER

TWENTY-ONE

Clark's was one of those "business diners" located in a building that had been squeezed in between two others more substantial ones. The local joke was that it used to be an alley that had been roofed over. Inside was only wide enough to accommodate the lunch counter and six two-seater tables lined to the long wall. The kitchen was behind a swinging door with window to prevent collisions. No one even wondered what might occupy the two upper floors. At lunch time, people packed into the small space, some eating in, most getting something to go. Terry and Sarah had beaten that crowd and were able to get a table, a coveted prize at Clark's.

Terry handed her one of the menus the management kept stuck between the napkin holder and the brick wall. They scanned the menu together, although he already knew what he'd order.

When the waitress came over, they ordered. Terry ate here so often that he knew her name, even without looking at her nametag. "Rose, I'll take the cheeseburger all the way with extra cheese, fries, and a large coke." He leaned across the table and confided in Sarah, "Their burgers are the best. You really ought to try one. You owe it to yourself."

Sarah made a point of looking at the menu one more time. "I'll order the chef salad, oil and vinegar dressing, ice tea, no sugar, extra lemon, please."

Terry shook his head. "You should have ordered the burgers. You would have done your taste buds a favor. I tell you they are the best." She just smiled. Something about her smile bothered Terry.

When the waitress brought their orders. She started to put the salad in front of Sarah. "No, HE gets the salad. I get the burger. It's a game we play. He orders for me and I order for him.

It keeps things interesting." She gave her sweetest smile and batted her eyes. "Isn't that right, Terry, dear?"

Rose showed a modicum of surprise when she heard, "dear."

He smiled and replied with a less than happy almost churlish, "Hey, that's right." She had a knack for boxing him into a corner. He felt like a leaf in a stream on a windy day. He knew what direction he was headed but had no control over what drove him there.

Terry leaned forward and in a perplexed whisper asked "What is the 'we order for each other? And this 'dear' business?"

Sarah put on the affectation of someone who has been emotionally hurt. "I thought the 'dear' was kind of cute, just to spice up your reputation. And the ordering for you, well, that was your fault. After all, you made the burgers sound so fantastic. I know you wouldn't want to deprive me of the experience. Don't forget that just last night you said that you need to get into shape." When Rose heard "last night" her eye brows went up. This conversation was getting interesting. She took extra time cleaning the table next to the couple. Sarah took a big bite of the hamburger. "I'm willing to risk my waistline. I'm making this sacrifice for your own good. Say, this burger is great. You were right." Terry noticed that her sacrifice didn't seem to be causing her any discomfort.

"The salad's very good" he had to admit after eating about half of it, even though his statement lacked enthusiasm. But it isn't my hamburger an unvoiced thought finished.

"My visitor was Mr. Overstreet, a labor leader. The man with him was a P.I. by the name of Camford. They were the ones behind these pictures of me in the paper, but not the attacks. Overstreet said he was trying to ruin my business." They both laughed at the reverse effect it had.

"Oh, that reminds me." Sarah said, between bites, "The El Dorado called. They said that the next time you plan to be there, let them know. They will comp you the evening. That does include a guest." She batted her lashes at him, again. "Just in case you wanted to take somebody in particular. They said their phone has been ringing off the hook since this morning's paper hit the streets."

The waitress came by with the bill. Terry looked at Sarah. "I'll have a hot fudge sundae" I may have been denied my burger, but I will have my dessert.

The waitress looked at Sarah then back to Terry. Sarah did a strategic fallback. She added, "And bring two spoons."

Clark's made their sundaes their hallmark dish. It was served in a cone-shaped bowl, a dab of sauce in the bottom, abundant ice cream covered with a warm, thick fudge, with an optional sprinkle of nuts. They refused to put whipped cream on top. "It only takes up room" was their reply when asked for whipped cream. People frequently asked for two spoons. Whether it was a sweltering summer day or frigid wintry weather, at least one person at Clark's ordered a sundae.

Terry and Sarah talked about the Wiresmith case. Sarah listened to him describe his client. From his description, she didn't like her. When he mentioned what Wiresmith had said about the women in her family, she stopped him. "But Mrs. Wiresmith isn't related to Bandy. She would be a step-grandmother. Why would she talk about her like she was a blood kin?"

Terry pondered the question while he took another bite of the sundae. He pretended like it was a new revelation to him, "Hmmm, good point. I missed that." He hadn't actually missed it. It just had slid past him for a moment, and he finally caught up with it. "I need to make another visit to the library and do a really deep background on her. I normally don't do backgrounds on my own clients, conflict of interest, you know. Thanks for the help. I'll tell you what: On the way back to the office, we'll stop in at Tony's, and I'll buy you a lollipop!" She knew that he was joking. He looked at her again. "No, I think, maybe gourmet chocolates, I'll let Tony decide."

The luncheon and the hot fudge sundae skirmish had left them both in a good mood as they walked back to the office. At the office, Terry got into the Red Rocket. Almost as an afterthought, he rolled down the window and asked: "Would you like to come along and help?" Sarah broke into a huge smile and ran to get in. At the library, Terry introduced Sarah to Emily Yardley before the two of them disappeared into the shelves to do their research. He divided their tasks up. He asked Sarah to investigate the estate. He wanted to explore Mrs. Wiresmith's history.

Sarah rejoined him an hour later. "I found two interesting facts. Old man Wiresmith left half his estate to his new wife and the other half to his granddaughter. The rider on the will was that if either of them predeceased the other before the final probating of the will, the entire estate would go to the survivor, no mention of a trust or such."

Terry wondered how she could get the information on the probate so fast. He told her what he had found. "The thing about the name of the widow, there was a Sandra McClain, but she ran a confidence game with her son in Denver, Colorado. She played a rich socialite, and he ran a phony charity. Don't know if it's the same person. That's all I've got." They got back to the office. Terry had to park in the spot closest to the road. True to his upbringing, he walked on the street side of the sidewalk.

He unconsciously reached for her hand, but before he could hold it, a car gunned its motor. Terry turned and saw a blue Buick aiming for their part of the sidewalk. He grabbed Sarah and spun towards the wall. The Buick took out two parking meters and sped away, one of its hubcaps rolling down the curb like it was chasing the car. The couple ended up in a heap with Sarah more or less in Terry lap.

Sarah's first comment was "You have ruined my hose. Now, I'll have to get a new pair." Her second was "But I notice that somehow you managed to get me on your lap. You are a roué!" Her normally flirtatious comment fell flat because he could feel the fear in her causing her to shake. He tightened his arms around her just a bit more, not sure whether he was trying to calm her or if it were a response to his fear, as well. The hug reassured her. The shoulder holster she felt because of it did not.

Back at the office, Sarah reached into the bottom desk drawer and pulled out a spare pair of nylons. She grabbed her purse. "I'll freshen up, and then we'll talk." While Sarah was in the bathroom, he called Al Hammod and told him about the car. He asked him to find out if anyone at the Wiresmith estate had a blue Buick. He hung up the phone just before Sarah re-entered her office.

She motioned to him to come into his office. "Let's talk in here." was all she said.

His mind had another shock. His office had changed. While they were at lunch, Artemis had come in and moved his desk and brought up a smaller one to occupy part of his office. Sarah saw his look. She squelched any protest from him. "You said that I could hire a temp. She has to use the outer office. That only left here for me and I only took a small corner."

He didn't remember saying anything about hiring a temp. Sarah continued, "I got the smallest office desk that I could find but still looked good. It is okay if I work in here with you, isn't it?" Terry looked at her. What could he say? He shrugged his shoulder. "Well, I guess so. It is only temporary." Somehow, it didn't feel temporary.

CHAPTER

TWENTY-TWO

There was a knock on the door and a timid "Hello?" and then a young girl's head stuck itself tentatively into the office. "My name is Anita. Anita Dorcet. I'm early. Then, holding up a brown paper bag, "I brought my lunch. I haven't had a chance to eat, yet." Anita was slightly taller than Sarah. Her brunette hair hung just below her shoulders. Her brown eyes seemed a tad too large which gave her a slightly bewildered air. Terry thought she looked sixteen instead of the twenty-one her ID said she was. He realized that the older he got, the younger everybody else looked.

Sarah went straight to her with an outstretched hand. "I'm Miss Dayton, and this is Mr. Rodgers." pointing towards him. "We are experiencing a sudden and possibly temporary upswing in interest in our agency." Terry noticed that Sarah had said "our agency" instead of "the agency."

Sarah continued, "Your job is receptionist. Answer the telephone and take messages. You will have an appointment calendar, but do not make appointments. It is there for you to know when we are not available. There are extra pads and pens in the desk. We can only guarantee a week of employment, but if circumstances dictate it might work into a full-time position. You will be working directly under me. We open at nine. Any questions?"

Anita looked at Sarah, "Is there someplace I can put my lunch?"

Sarah took Anita into the inner office and showed her the new refrigerator she had bought. "You can use this one, and the powder room is over there." and pointed to the closed door. Terry started to feel like Sarah's refrigerator, and other changes pushed him towards a mere corner of his office. "If you want, go ahead and eat your lunch at the desk. Normally, we don't do that, but you're hungry and right now there is a lull in activity." In his own agency, he no longer had his own space or any say on what went on.

Sarah decided that Anita needed an orientation on Confidential's office practices. Terry stopped her. "Miss Dayton, please, stay." Terry needed a moment of privacy with Sarah in his office. "We have something to discuss about that case." Anita excused herself. She grabbed her lunch and closed the connecting door. Terry got out the bag from his desk and handed it to her.

Terry was terse and more intense than she had ever seen him. "This is a more dangerous than you think. To get to the bottom of this, I have to go alone. I don't have enough solid evidence to go to the police. I will be facing killers, of that I am sure. I'm taking you to a priest I know. I think he can keep you safe a lot better than I could. I want you to have this."

Sarah refused to accept what he said. When she saw what was inside, she looked crest-fallen. "I don't like guns and I thought you didn't either, but I notice that you're wearing one today." She didn't like the idea of handling or wearing a gun. She knew that she could not possibly be the target of anyone's plot. Even the people who handled her eccentricities back in Kansas City liked her. "It can't be that bad if you say that the priest could keep me safe. I don't think a priest would want me to have a gun on church property. It might not even be legal. Besides, you told me that guns make people feel like doing something stupid."

Terry tried to get her to analyze the events of the last few days. "Look, someone is try-ing to kill one or both of us. They're amateurs. That makes them stupid. Stupid makes them dangerous. A pro wouldn't have missed at the Blue Ohio and rags in the engine or running someone down on the street, that's the sort of rubbish you find in those dollar novels in the desperation piles at book stores. Using the same blue Buick is definitely bush league. They had three misses but they might get lucky.

"This pistol," he pulled the gun out of the bag. He showed her the semi-automatic, "is my old back up gun. It's small and might kill someone, but it's doubtful. It's got a round in the chamber and a full magazine. The safety is on. If you get into trouble, take the safety off by doing this. There is a round in the chamber" he repeated. "Just point and keep pulling the trigger until it stops. More than likely, you'll scare whoever away, rather than causing any actual bodily harm."

She crossed her arms. "You know, they could be after you, and I'm just an innocent bystander. Besides, I am not going to carry a gun, particularly on my thigh. What am I supposed to do? Say to the attacker, 'Excuse me for a moment while I reach up under my skirt? I have to get my gun, so be patient'. I will not carry that and you cannot make me."

Terry lost his temper. He hadn't lost his temper in years. He might have exploded at events a few times, but not lost his temper because a person wouldn't listen to him. Maybe, this was the first time in years that he cared enough about anything to get mad. He snapped the pistol in the holster. Then he pushed Sarah back on the sofa. Like the reverse of a wedding garter scene, he expanded the elastic and slid it up her leg and unto her thigh. "There! And don't let me catch you without it. It's important to me that I know you are protected."

He grabbed her arm and pulled her to her feet and through his doorway. In the outer office, without looking at Anita, he said, "Call Mrs. Wiresmith. Tell her that I'm coming over. Her number should be on the desk."

As they left the office, Sarah shouted over her shoulder, "Keep working, Anita, I don't know when we'll be back. I'll try to call you," and with her free hand closed the door behind them. As the door closed, Anita said to herself, "My, things sure happen fast around here!"

CHAPTER

TWENTY-THREE

On the way to St. Ignatius, he kept his eyes on the road and his hands on the wheel. She kept her hands folded on her purse in her lap. Terry tried to figure out all the possible outcomes. He needed to bring a murderer to justice. He just couldn't figure out how Sarah fit into the equation. He knew for certain that she was in danger.

Sarah remained quiet for another reason. She didn't know what was happening so she hadn't formed a response. She did intend to get rid of the pistol as soon as Terry couldn't see. Somehow or another, this was not working out like she thought it would. She knew that she could never use anything deadly against another human being. She thought that maybe when all of this was over, she had better go back to

K.C. She could just chock all of this up to another one of her adventures.

At St. Ignatius, they went looking for Father Peterson. Sarah followed only because she didn't know what else to do. They found Father Peterson in the fellowship hall. The priest noticed a sense of urgency he hadn't seen in Terry for years. "Hey, Frank, I've got a volunteer for your snack program." He turned to Sarah. "You'll be serving Hydrox and Hawaiian punch to a group of school dropouts and gang bangers."

Father Peterson never liked the way Terry characterized his "kids," as he called them. He did notice the unfamiliar bulge in Terry's jacket. He knew that only the direst circumstances would make Terry break his word and carry a gun, but said nothing. "Now, Terry, you know I can't afford Hydrox, but I do have some generic cookies and Kool-Aid, for anyone who stops by, even private eyes."

Terry pulled out his wallet and dug in it for some money to give the priest. Frank refused to accept it. All the priest said was, "Friends." While he was trying to make Terry take it back, the picture of Amanda Setrap fell out on to the table in front of the priest.

The priest picked it up and looked at it. "Now where did you get such a sweet picture of Janey?' He turned to Sarah, "Are you related to her? You look like sisters or cousins."

Terry couldn't believe what he had just heard. "Frank, do you know this woman?'" The statement about going to find some young men. Maybe St. Ignatius was where she had gone to help, not find, young men at some other club. Either the waitress or Sarah had gotten it wrong.

"Of course,' the priest chortled. "I even have her picture in what you call my rouges' gallery. If you would have looked last time you were here, you would have seen it. Her full name is Amanda Jane Setrap. She goes by Janey. If you want to meet her, she'll be in this afternoon to help with snacks. A fine, young woman."

For Terry, this information made all the dots form a picture. For Sarah, it made her decide to stay and meet this woman. She hoped that she could prove to Terry that she could help him on this case. She just couldn't figure out why it was important to prove it to him. She didn't know how meeting Janey would be of any consequence, but she planned to meet her.

Outside, Terry got into his car. He reached out from the driver's seat and grabbed the priest's arm. "Frank, I know I don't have to say this, but watch her. She's in danger and doesn't believe it. I gave her a gun. I wanted you to know. You are the only person I trust to protect her." Terry started the Rust Bucket as Frank put a priestly hand on his shoulder, "On my word as a man of the cloth and your friend. I'll do all that I can."

He wondered why his friend needed his help. He was glad that after twenty years, he had started to care. He didn't like the idea of a firearm in his church, but, for Terry, he'd allow it. In his mind, he thought that maybe this young woman was the person God had sent to redeem his friend. Maybe, his friend was the person this young woman needed to meet some deficiency in her own life. Time and prayer would let him know.

Father Peterson went back to the fellowship hall to find Sarah. He told her that Terry was under the church's protection and God had a strong arm and that Terry had promised to come back for her when it was all over. Sarah had other plans. She wasn't going to be passive in all of this. She decided that once she had a chance to talk with this Setrap person, she would do something other than the traditional serve cookies and juice. She remembered back in college how she and her friends had promised themselves never to be passive and submissive. "Father, do you have someplace I can safely keep my purse and" in a whisper, "Where is the ladies'?" Her first task was to get rid of the gun.

He pointed to a restroom with the international symbol on it "There, and you can put your purse in any cabinet. You and Janey are the only ones who will be allowed to the kitchen. I haven't seen Terry this concerned about someone else since" Sarah's interest shifted to what the priest was saying. "Well, let's just say 'ever.' I know he's worried. It's the only time I've ever known him to break his vow to never touch a gun again. You know, young lady, you must be really special. I think you might be the one who…" The priest forced himself to stop before he might reveal a confidence. The priest's statement was cotton candy to her curiosity: sweet but not satisfying.

Sarah went to the restroom and removed the gun and holster and put them in her purse. She went to the kitchen and put her purse under the sink, behind the steel wool pads and the drain cleaner. She heard a noise at the kitchen door and saw someone who did resemble her a bit walk in. The woman went to the pantry and put on an apron.

"Hi, I'm Janey. You must be new here."

"I'm Sarah. I'm supposed to stay here until a friend gets back." She answered. She added with only a modicum of enthusiasm, "Father Peterson put me in charge of Kool-Aid. He didn't tell me how much to make."

"Oh, once the kids get here, just keep making it until we either run out of kids or out of Kool-Aid. Usually, we run out of Kool-Aid first." As if on command, the afterschool masses started arriving. They were laughing and pushing each other. They seemed to enjoy the fellowship hall. To Sarah, the fellowship hall looked shabby, like worn out jeans with patches. The tables wobbled, and some had plywood screwed to the tops to cover up old holes. The chairs looked rusty and unstable. To the children from the neighborhood, the fellowship hall spoke of peace and caring. The cookies and Kool-Aid was a nice snack, but the safety and unity made this place a priceless sanctuary.

The group seemed to be made up of young people who looked years older than they actually were. The streets can age a person, fast. Sarah guessed that they ranged from about eleven to sixteen. Some of them wore the same colors. Others sported tattoos. Some bore scars like medals of past battles. One boy displayed the scars of his bullet wounds, bragging about the gang's street fight where he got them.

Father Peterson came in and the atmosphere in the room changed. As the numbers increased the kids sorted themselves out into groups according to which gang with which they aligned themselves. Sarah had seen gangs before, but these were less volatile and the language was much cleaner or less vulgar, depending on one's point of view. Some of the boys were helping Janey put out cookies and some fresh fruit. Father Frank insisted that fruit be available for the youngest kids. One of the leaders, Alphonzo, had the line organized.

"I'm amazed." She told him, "I was expecting this to be a bit more, well, hostile."

Alphonzo overheard her comment to Janey. "Father Peterson don't want no cussing or fighting in front of ladies or the little kids; so we try real hard not to cuss at St. Ignatius'. And he told us that if anybody starts anything, ain't nobody in that group can come back for a week unless he loses his colors. And Miss Janey, there, she don't got to do this. It's not like the court ordered her to do community service or anything. All the gangs here decided she's under our protection and St. Ignatius is like Switzerland."

He stuck out a friendly hand. "Hi, my name's Alphonzo. Did the courts tell you to come here too?"

Sarah shook his hand. "I'm Sarah Dayton. No, no court order. My boss wanted me to stay here. He asked Father Peterson and he said that I'd be safe."

"Lady, I guess that you're under our protection, too." He turned to the line, "Hey, let's get started. Little kids first. Everybody line up!" Then over his shoulder to Sarah, "We need more Kool-Aid, lady." After that, her street name was "Kool-Aid Lady."

Sarah went back to the kitchen and kept creating more and more Kool-Aid, always about one pitcher behind the demand. She had a big metal spoon for stirring, but had to get a fork to break up the sugar that had coalesced into a solid block. The snacks that the church provided were from local businessmen, but they didn't always donate their freshest stock. In this part of town, stale cookies and lumpy sugar was considered a treat. She focused on her drink preparation so intently that she didn't see the blue Buick pull up behind the fellowship hall. She didn't see the man with the gun get out. She was only vaguely aware of the kitchen door opening and closing. It was Charles.

A hand went over her mouth and a gun to her back. "Miss Setrap, you are coming with me. Please, don't make any noise or I will have to hurt you here where there are all of these children. Others might be injured. Mrs. Wiresmith is taking care of Mr. Rodgers. After that, we will take care of you." If Charles thought that his statement would make Sarah cower into obedience, he was wrong. The statement only informed her that she didn't have anything to lose since he told her that her death was already planned.

Her first reaction was to try to explain he had the wrong person, but his hand was clamped so tightly just breathing was difficult. She could feel panic stealing her ability to reason.

In the struggle, her hand closed around the fork. She raised her arm a bit and brought the fork down hard on the man's thigh. The pain caused him to cry out and release her. He dropped his gun and grabbed his leg. She tore out of the kitchen and into the great room. Her foot caught the gun and sent it skittering off in some unseen direction.

"Man! Kitchen! Gun!" was the best she could gasp out and pointed at the door.

Anger had overridden Charles' reason and he chased after her. As he came through the door, Janey hit him in the face with a heavy aluminum tray on which dozens of cookie had been sitting but, now, flew through the air, scattering all over the place.

As he staggered a bit, he yelled a profane epithet at the woman. For a moment, nobody moved. This man had violated Father Peterson's first rule. He got up and slapped Janey Setrap. That violated the gangs' first rule. Janey was under their protection. The gangs moved as a group to action.

Suddenly, pandemonium broke out among the teens, and several of the older boys from various gangs were attacking Charles, or to their way of thinking, protecting Janey. Each gang determined not to let another gang be the one with bragging rights to how this invader was dealt with. Fists, feet, and a couple of chains soon had Charles curled into a ball. The only thing that saved the man was the appearance of Father Peterson plowing his way through the mass of violence that had erupted in his domain.

The group spontaneously pulled back into a circle and let the Father through. Alphonzo whispered to Sarah out of the corner of his mouth "You'll tell Father that we didn't start it and we didn't cuss in front of the kids or you ladies, too much, won't you?" Any other time she might have laughed. Now she just nodded solemnly, still shook up.

"Don't let the man get away." Father Peterson instructed the group. "I've got to call the police." His statement was meant as much as a warning as anything else. Several of the kids left with the mention of the police, which he understood. Alphonzo and a few other gang leaders stayed. Two rival gang members whose weight showed an over-fondness of desserts sat on him, one on his back, and the other on his feet. They divided the money that they found in his wallet. Charles was too terrified to do much and said nothing. The priest surveyed the situation and considered it under control. He made the two young men give him the money, which he returned to the wallet.

He turned to the two women who were trying to recover themselves. "Ladies, they'll want to talk to you, too." The priest left to go to the church office.

Sarah went into the kitchen and searched for the gun with which he threatened her.

She found it under the stove. She took a broom and pushed it out. Her next step was to go to Janey.

"Janey, this man tried to kidnap me because he thought I was you. Take this gun and give it to the police. When they ask about me, just tell them I work for Terry Rodgers at Confidential Investigations. Right now, I've got to get to the Wiresmith estate. She plans to kill Terry. Tell the police to go there." She turned to the group. "And if any of you are asked, you never saw me. I was in the kitchen the whole time." That was a scenario that any of the gangs could live with. They didn't know why she didn't want police to know too much about her, but they didn't care. When it came to the police, they didn't see or hear anything.

She couldn't afford the risk of being delayed by police wanting to question her.

Sarah ran into the kitchen and retrieved her purse and then hurried out the door. She looked right and left, wondering about how she could get to the Wiresmith estate and fast. She spotted the Buick. She ran over to it and looked through the window. Great! The keys are in it. She jumped in. Her legs barely reached the pedals. She moved the seat forward while she fired up the engine and threw it into reverse. She backed out of the lot, hitting a "Pitch In" anti-litter waste can scattering trash all over the church lot. Then she jammed the transmission into drive and jumped the curb. The acceleration pushed her back into the seat. She dodged in and out of traffic and ran what lights she had to. While she was driving, she tried to retrieve the gun from her purse but couldn't. If she survived her driving, it was a cinch she'd be pulling police cars in her wake.

CHAPTER

TWENTY-FOUR

Terry pulled up to the front of the Wiresmith house. He slammed the door of the Dodge and took the front steps two at a time. This time he beat on the door. A very serene looking Mrs. Wiresmith answered the door.

"Why Mr. Rodgers, won't you come in." Her satin voice demonstrated no sign of stress. "Charles took the message from your receptionist that you were coming over. I am sorry that he wasn't here to let you in." He wondered where Charles was, but immediately refocused his mind on this woman.

She continued, "Why don't we sit in the garden where we can enjoy this lovely weather? I'm afraid we will have to use mugs instead of fine china. I made the tea, myself. We are all by ourselves, today. I gave my staff the day off. I felt that they deserved a day off. We needed a lot of privacy." When they got to the room at the end of the hall, coffee and tea was ready.

"No, thank you, Mrs. Wiresmith, I came to tell you that the game is over and you've lost. I know you tried to kill me and the woman you thought was your step granddaughter. I think that I can prove that the death of your husband came from being served Zigadenus venenosus. You used his previous heart attack and, I assume, an unscrupulous doctor to eliminate the need for an autopsy. I suggest that you and your son were plotting to siphon off many of the estate's assets and were afraid that your step-granddaughter would either ask for her share of the estate, or realize what you had planned and alert the authorities. She might even start wondering about her grandfather's death."

She poured herself a cup of coffee. "Are you sure you don't want a cup? I must say, Mr. Rodgers, as a detective, you have certainly been a big disappointment to me. I looked around for the worst private detective in the city. Several of you colleagues mentioned you, by name. They said that you were a has-been and a bum, a drunken sot, a dipsomaniac. When you came to my home, I knew immediately that you were all that they said you were and less. I made sure that the information I gave you was insufficient for you to find my step granddaughter. I wanted you to run into blind allies and false leads. But, unfortunately, you still found Amanda."

"Calling her your secretary did not fool me for an instant. Even from where he was watching, Charles recognized her as you were leaving that roadhouse, the Blue O, or whatever it was. When you came by the other day, instead of calling, you alerted my staff that you existed. Even today, I gave them all the day off, just like I did the first time. I didn't want anyone to know that I hired you to find Amanda. That ridiculous rider on the will. Like her grandfather, both of you will be killed. For my husband, it was an induced heart attack. For you...I think 'You attacked my granddaughter, being a lecherous clubber that the papers demonstrated you to be. When she rebuffed you, you shot her. I happened along in time to shoot you but not to save my precious Amanda. No one knows that you are here. And the reason I brought you to this room is I can see the road from it. Oh, good, I see Charles' Buick. He is bringing Amanda here. Shall we go meet him?"

"No, Mrs. Wiresmith, because one way or another this ends here. Either you and your son come with me to the police or you won't be around to read tomorrows obits."

Terry didn't worry. He knew that he was out of shape, but didn't think that this seventy-something, skinny woman posed any threat, plus he had his gun in his shoulder holster.

"Pity. I do so love reading obituaries, but only other people's." She set her coffee cup down and in the same fluid motion came up with a pistol that she had secreted next to the easy chair. Terry cursed himself for not antici-pating this type of trouble and for violating his own rules. Rule number one: Call the police. They have guns. Rule two: If you plan to use a gun, pull yours first!

Her voice and smile continued to be conge-nial. "It is old." She nodded towards the gun. "Let me assure it that it functions quite well and, at this range is quite deadly. Now, Mr.

Rodgers, please, leave your gun behind and accompany me to the garden where I'm sure I can find some material for tomorrow's obituary column. I'm sure that you'll enjoy the fresh air rather than being cooped up in a stuffy old house. Plus, it makes the mess easier to clean up. I'll make sure that when the police get here, they'll find your gun."

Terry pulled out his thirty-eight and laid it very carefully on the floor next to the chair.

He stood up and walked over to the French doors. He put his palms on the glass. The purpose of his actions were not lost on Mrs. Wire smith. "Go ahead, open them, and don't worry about finger prints. I'm sure you can appreciate the need to keep a home in this area absolutely display ready. I'm sure that with all the activity that will be around here, I should have plenty of time to make sure that they disappear. I'll make sure that the maid cleans the door, thoroughly."

They stepped outside. Terry was forming a plan in his mind. "Hey, Sandy, you do realize that your plan is stupid and only an imbecile would think it would work." Terry was trying to make her mad, and he hoped that, by calling her by her first name, he could distract her long enough for him to make a move any move.

Sandra Wiresmith responded, "Ah, Mr. Rodgers, rudeness so ill becomes you, but what can one expect from someone who displays his lack of culture so readily. You should take a course in deportment or a remedial one in manners. Oh, but you won't be around to sign up for one. Pity." She hadn't risen to his bait and showed no change in demeanor. Terry was taken back by the total lack of emotion in her voice. The word "psychopath" came to mind.

He couldn't tell if she were a stone cold killer or if this ultra politeness was an affectation that fit the high society role she was so used to playing. Whatever the truth might be, he was sure that in a matter of a few moments, the answer wouldn't matter to him. She was the writer and director of this play, and he didn't think that he was going to like the final scene. His mind kept turning, trying to find some way of creating an alternative ending. The only thing out of place came to the forefront of his senses. He swore he could hear running water.

In her grand play, she had forgotten about one of the players, Bill. She assumed that everyone would take off for the impromptu holiday. She had given all her staff the day off, but he was dedicated to his plants, especially the new ones he planted, yesterday. He was there watering some of the new bushes. He was so scared when he saw Mrs. Wiresmith with a gun that he threw the hose away and ran. When he tossed the hose into the air, a stream of water hit Mrs. Wiresmith in the face. She sputtered and shook her head. Terry took the opportunity to attack.

He hit her hard and she fell. He thought the blow would knock the fight out of this seventy-something woman. Any man who had to street fight knew that first, you knock the wind out of an opponent. Never go for the head unless you have some type of club. The head's too hard. She should have stayed down, but he forgot one thing about women: they fight dirty.

She came at him all fang and claws. She was hitting, biting and scratching, all at the same time. The calm façade had crumbled. Each kick or scratch she gave him increased the violence of her attacks. In one of her attacks, she got him in his in the eye causing it to water so much that seeing was difficult. Terry was losing ground. Another raking scratch near his eye and across his cheek made him back up until he had no cover.

Now she seemed more like an animal. She crouched down and was hissing as she slowly circled him. Out of the corner of his eye, he caught movement. At first he was afraid it might be Charles. He may have delayed his fate but he hadn't escaped it. Then he realized it was too small, moving too fast. With a vengeance that would make a Fury from Greek mythology proud, a woman leapt on Wiresmith's back. She fought dirty, too.

He couldn't make out who was there for a moment or two. His eye cleared a bit. Wild cats in mortal combat was his first reaction. Terry had been trained in hand to hand in the Army. He had been in his share of bar brawls and no hold barred street fights, but this fight was one of the most vicious he had seen. He couldn't even follow or describe what happened. He recognized Mrs. Wiresmith as one of the wild cats. He identified Sarah as the other one. The sounds of tearing fabric interrupted the screams and profanities. The ball of twin furies rolled into a flower bed. Some of the plants were ripped out of the ground. Mrs. Wiresmith managed to stand up. Sarah pushed her over and into a couple of rose bushes. She continued the fight. Both women unaware or simply heedless of the rose bushes' counter-attack with its thorny canes. Suddenly, the fight was over and Sarah was straddling Mrs. Wiresmith using her knees to pin down Wiresmith's upper arms. The words coming out of Mrs. Wiresmith were not those of high society, but dredged up for the depths of the gutter. There were some words Rodger had never heard and had no idea of their meaning. Suddenly she stopped spouting out words with an "Urk."

From somewhere Sarah had produced the gun Mrs. Wiresmith had recently pointed at him. She pushed it into Wiresmith's throat, just at the "V" where the trachea and clavicle girdle meet.

In a cold, dispassionate voice, Sarah said, "Honey, I've been reading how the new fashion involves body piercing and I'd love to try practicing it on you. So just move or even breathe funny and I'll start the piercing." The wide-eyed, panicked look showed that she believed Sarah. Off in the distance, the sound of approaching police sirens were heard.

The police arrived and took the gun from Sarah. The two women tried to re-engage in their death match. It took eight officers to keep them apart. The lead officer took the initial reports, the gardener told them what he had seen. As they cuffed Mrs. Wiresmith and led her to a patrol car, Bill was assessing the damage to the plants, talking to each one like injured victims, collateral damage from the violent fight.

Sarah sat down on a step, visibly shaking. She pushed her hair out off her forehead. Her blouse was torn and dirty. Some of the scratches on her arms were seeping a bit of blood. One side of her skirt had been ripped up to the thigh. Among her skirt's other battles scars were a few missing button; so that one questionable button held it on. She looked down and straightened her skirt just a bit. "Crap!" She looked up at Terry. "I ruined my last pair of hose." She began shaking from the adrenaline. Terry sat next to her and put his arm around her.

After the police were finished with them, they walked to Terry's car. Terry looked at her. "I'm glad you came. You were a Godsend."

Sarah gave a short laugh. "Your friend said that God would protect you, that God had a strong arm of protection. But I'm the one who got here."

Terry looked at her. "And how do you think that you got here just in time? You are my guardian angel, at least for today. Maybe, God did send you." Terry surprised himself. He had said it and, right then he believed it.

Behind them, Bill, the gardener, tended his injured plants. He was replanting them and telling them that they'd soon be all better. He had a few negative things to say about Mrs. Wiresmith and even though he knew that Sarah had saved Terry's life, he still gave her a few unkind words about what she did to his plants.

CHAPTER

TWENTY-FIVE

The next three weeks were a bit of a blur. Police statements and depositions were taken. It took both Sarah and Terry to convince Amanda Jane to take her grandfather's money. They focused on the good she could do. The final point that convinced her was that if she didn't come forward, the state would get the estate and swallow it whole. She moved into the mansion and treated the help like her grandfather had done. She did insist on keeping her day job at Cranwell, Cranwell, and Muzzey, Attorneys at Law.

Father Peterson's program became the media's darling for about three days. Its funding was more secure thanks to an anonymous donor with the initials "AJS." At least, that way, Janey found a good use for her grandfather's sizable fortune. Although she did keep enough to make sure that she and her staff were comfortable.

Things at Confidential Investigations slowed down, but only to the point that he could take cases with a touch of class. Anita was told she could stay until the end of the month and then they would re-evaluate the situation. Everything seemed to be going well. Then that Friday morning came.

Terry showed up at the McCrary building carrying two bouquets and wearing a suit. He had decided to be a professional, again. His watch read eight thirty, and he was opening the office door. He wanted to surprise both women with flowers as a special thank-you for being great assets. Life is good! When he walked inside, someone was waiting. On the couch sat Sarah with a suitcase on the floor, in front of her.

"I've decided to go back to Kansas City.," she said flatly. "That's where my responsibilities lie. I've got a life back there. My plane leaves in about an hour. I wanted you to hear it from me. Will you take me to the airport?" She didn't look at him, but straight at his office door. "I won't be coming back except for the trial."

He felt gut-punched, but what could he do. "Sure, no problem. You had to go back some-time." An obviously forced smile appeared on his face, "That's where your life is. You have to go back. I understand. No problem." I'm repeating myself like some idiot. Get a grip. She's young and wants to be around her friends. He rummaged around in Anita's desk looking for pen and paper. He grabbed an old envelope from the trash. For some reason, he didn't see the memo pad on her desk. "I'll just leave a note for Anita and we can leave. I wouldn't want her to worry when she got here and nobody shows up." He picked up her suitcase. The walk to the elevator was long and silent. He never liked elevators. This elevator ride seemed like a descent into lowest realms of Dante's Inferno to him. On the way to the airport, he turned on the radio just to have the noise chase the quiet away.

"..And that was the number thirty-one hit for the year 1982, 'Always on my Mind' by Willie Nelson. We're reaching way back for our next hit." The sound of a rusty hinge to accent the antiquity of the song came over the speakers. "All the way to 1968. Peter, Paul, and Mary's 'Leaving on a Jet Plane.'" Their hands collided as they both reached to turn the radio off.

At the airport, she checked in her luggage. She heard her flight being called. "Walk me to the gate?" He shrugged his shoulders and walked with her. There was a lot that he'd like to say to her, but, since she was leaving, none of it mattered anymore. She was busy trying to think of some way to make the leaving not as sad as she felt. She felt like she was abandoning a friend. At the gate, she whispered, "This is your last chance to frisk me to see if I stole that holster you had made for me." He turned bright red. She tapped him on the nose, "You are so easy."

She realized this was the last time that she would see this man who had found her and whose life she had saved. She knew that there was one last thing she could do to him. Suddenly, she grabbed his head. She kissed him, the sort of kiss that let the entire airport know he wasn't her father or an uncle, or even a cousin. She couldn't have explained why she kissed him, only that it seemed like the thing to do. Then she went through the gate, turned around and wave one last, small wave. He waited until he watched her plane take off.

He didn't go back to the office. Instead, he went to a liquor store he had passed on the way to the airport and bought three bottles of the cheapest whiskey they had. The drunk he was planning did not deserve the respect of a decent whiskey. Then he went to his own apartment. He got out a tumbler and filled it up. The phone rang, and he ignored it. "This is to celebrate finding Miss Sarah with an "h" Dayton and took a drink. "And this is for bringing a murderer to justice." Then he downed the rest of the glass. The phone rang again. He imagined that it must be Anita. He ripped the cord out of the wall. He went on toasting everything including the icemaker that his freezer didn't have. He kept on until his brain couldn't feel any longer. The last thing he remembered was saluting the fact that he was the miserable failure that Wiresmith and his colleagues had said. He agreed with them. Oblivion covered him.

CHAPTER

TWENTY-SIX

An insistent alarm kept buzzing. What is that? Oh, yeah. Alarm. I must have set it last night. What day is it? He stumbled out of bed. According to the radio program, it was Wednesday. The apartment gave every evidence that he had spent the weekend here, plus the missing Monday and Tuesday. Empty bottles littered the floor. I must have ordered in. I have to get it together and get to the office. Sarah had gotten him back into the habit of going to the office looking professional. He took a long hot shower and then shaved off five days' worth of beard. The noise of the electric razor sent shock waves through his brain like a punishment for his self-destructive excess. They continued to ricochet around in his skull even after he had finished shaving. By the time he left his apartment, it was moving towards ten o'clock. When he went to get his car, the hangover kept him from recognizing it. It took him a minute or two to remember that Doug had repainted the "Rust Bucket" and it looked like the mint fresh "Rocket" of twenty years ago. "Or maybe I just want things to go back to the way they had been, before..." He reached in the glove compartment and found some of the aspirin he had gotten for Sarah. He started the car, popped the aspirin and chewed. Then he pointed the Rocket toward the office. Like an old horse, it seemed to know the way there by itself, which was good. He felt in no condition to drive.

On the way to the office, he stopped for coffee at his favorite diner. The pimple-faced teenager at the counter asked "What can I get for you, today, sir?

"Coffee, black" he managed to order. "Yes, sir, would you like cream or sugar with that?"

He glared at the young man. "Coffee, black. That means no sugar, no cream. Just coffee in a cup. Do you understand or is English an alien concept to you?" Normally, he had no use for customers who are jerks, but, today, he was a jerk with all the options, and he didn't feel bad about it. Actually, he felt bad about everything and wanted the world to join him.

"Yes, sir." and poured the coffee into a Styrofoam cup.

I can't even get coffee in a real cup anymore. The whole world's going to the dogs

He finally made it to his building. As he walked down the hall towards his office. He noticed that the new tenants had moved into the office next door. Great! Another change to show life is passing me by. When he got to his office, coffee in hand, he heard the phone ring. He started to fumble for keys out of habit. A voice in the office said "Confidential Investigations" For a moment, he thought it was Sarah. Then mused, "No, not Sarah. That's Anita. I guess this is her last week. I'll give her the rest of the week off with pay. Then I'll tear that phone out of the wall, too." He walked in.

Anita was finishing a message. When she was done, she looked up. "Good morning, Mr. Rodgers. We've been worried about..." She saw him. "Oh! My! God! What happened to you? You look like road kill." She was trying to hand him an envelope with his name on it. He recognized Sarah's handwriting. It looked like it might be a greeting card or something. His mind was still fuzzy, and his head still hurt. Most of all, he didn't want to deal with anything connected with Sarah. He couldn't handle it, not now, maybe not ever.

"Thanks for the update. Why don't you take the rest of the day, no, make it the week off with pay." Anita's confusion seemed to increase. She looked back over her shoulder like she had to double check his instructions with someone else.

"Don't you think you'd better check with your office manager before you start getting free and easy with my employee and our budget." a very familiar voice said.

Standing in the doorway to his office was Sarah. She was leaning with her hand against the doorframe. He didn't know that when he didn't come back from the airport, Anita got concerned, especially with his telephone out of order. So when he didn't come in on Monday, she decided to call Sarah.

The only thing she could think to do was call the telephone company and get numbers that had been called from the office and hope one of them would help. A couple of them were to the eight one six area code. She left a message for Sarah at a place called S.D. Enterprises. Sarah finally returned her call on Tuesday.

Sarah put her hands on her hips and a smile on her face. Her smile started chasing things in his mind. "I go away for three days and everything goes to rack and ruin. You need to get to your office and get to work." Terry couldn't stop smiling.

Anita answered another call. "Confidential Investigations" pause "No, sir, we no longer handle that type of case. We are referring all such cases to Mr. Camford. Yes, sir, you can find him in the yellow pages."

"Oh, that's a nice touch," he said.

"In your office, now. Your cases won't handle themselves, you know! Thanks to your long weekend, we are several days behind on the new cases. We don't know about you, but the rest of us in this office would like to get paid, so go bring in some cash!" was her only reaction.

Terry suddenly realized he had no office. The frosted glass now read "Conference Room." Sarah motioned to him with her finger. He followed. The conference room had a nice table and chairs. The Mr. Coffee sat on a table near the window as did some pastries. Next to the table was the refrigerator Sarah had purchased. A new door had been cut into the "Conference Room," on it was a sign "Sarah Dayton Office Manager."

He continued to follow her into her office, an office that reflected Sarah's good taste. On the wall where she could see it was framed two cards: the ten of clubs and the Queen of Hearts. Under them read "The Winning Hand." On the desk sat one of those multiple lined phones and a bouquet of flowers. He read the card and was surprised he had sent them to her. Was it one of her jokes or did he call the florist in his drunken stupor and have the flowers sent to the office? There were two other solid wood doors. He finally noticed the third door that was open. It read "T. Rodgers, Investigator. Through it, he could see his office and a door to the hall.

She led him by the hand through two doors into her office.

"That is our private bathroom. Keep it clean! The old one is for clients." She opened the other door. "This is our closet. It has a small refrigerator and two complete changes of clothes for each of us. Just in case. I had to guess at your size." She gave a warm smile.

It must have been the aspirin, but Terry's headache had disappeared.

Then they went to his office. It had a private entrance from the hall. The frosted glass in the door had nothing on it except the old "Private Office" lettering from some long-ago occupant. A new leather couch replaced his old one, but the old Underwood still sat on his desk next to his old phone. The answering machine was neatly wrapped up and thrown in the waste basket. "This time, don't retrieve it. Let it go live with all the other answering machines."

Later on, when she couldn't see, he would rescue it, take it home and put it in his closet.

They walked back to the conference room where Anita had made coffee and put out Danishes. He noticed a shelf that held three mugs. One read "Anita." The next one read "Terry: Me Boss You Not: That's Why." The third read "Sarah: Be reasonable. Do it my way." He tried a cup of Anita's coffee. It was drinkable but just barely.

"Give her time." Sarah whispered, "She's young and just learning. Better be nice to her," she warned.

He raised his cup to Anita and said "MMM, good." She smiled and returned to her desk.

Terry could contain himself no longer. He gave her a long hug. She just stood there, her arms down at her sides. Her lack of response surprised him. He had to ask in spite of her apparent indifference. "I thought you moved back to Kansas City, for good. What brought you back here?

"I had to make sure that the remodeling of your office was done correctly. I know that you felt pushed out by all the other changes and needed your own spot. Besides when Anita called me, worried about you since you had disappeared, I realized that someone has to take care of you, and poor Anita is too young for the job. Or maybe, I just really liked it here." She looked around quickly. "You know, the work environment.

By the way, you need to learn that hugs are physical contact that can constitute sexual harassment in the workplace. There will be no sexual harassment allowed here," as she made a sweeping motion around the room.

Then she winked at him, "That's what our private offices are for."

Terry blushed a bright red. Sarah smiled and tapped him on the nose. "You are so easy." She had decided to make a game of how often she could make him flustered with, "innocent" comments.

Terry patted her on the head, "Okay, brat, I guess we better get to work." He walked into his new office. He left the door open enough to keep an eye on her, to prove she wasn't just a hoped-for illusion. She looked up and saw him and started humming Desperado." He pretended to be reviewing his appointments but mentally was a thousand miles away.

She is my Queen of Hearts. Maybe this relationship will work out, after all.

"Miss Dayton, would you come into my office to discuss the day's itinerary?" Sarah walked into his office and closed the door.

Biography
James Love

James Love comes from a long line of story tellers. A Minister and retired teacher – James honed his skills by relating historical anecdotes to his students. A native of Missouri, he currently lives in Florida. When he's not writing he enjoys leather working and blacksmithing. His knowledge of other cultures and history lend to the verisimilitude of his stories.

Watch for the next book in this series!

Smoke & Mirrors

Life has a way of throwing curves when you're expecting a fastball. When Sarah misunderstands a past case, Terry ends up on the receiving end of her anger. She even takes a case of her own from a mysterious, dark eyed stranger.

His case brings him face-to-face with drug smuggling.

Her case leads to a boyfriend for her and a girlfriend for Terry.

When her boyfriend is murdered, she is the prime suspect and the focus of close surveillance.

He'll need help from Sarah, old friends with law enforcement and the D.A.'s office to unravel clues and solve the case.